The Inn

at

Silver Springs

Also by Tima S. Dowding

Silver Springs Collection

Silver Mountain

Silver Creek

The Inn at Silver Springs

Coming Soon...

The Lodge at Silver Lake

The Inn
at
Silver Springs

By Tima S. Dowding

Book Three of the Silver Springs Collection

Written and Edited by Tima S. Dowding
Cover Art by Tima S. Dowding

Dedication

To Mike Drummond, who has been my best friend since we met in 1989. You are the one person who knows me better than anyone, even myself and after everything we have been through over the years, our friendship has never wavered. We have proven to everyone that a friendship like ours can and will last forever and I will always cherish what we have…

To Usha M Uthayan, who unexpectedly lost her battle to cancer in May of this year. You were my friend, confidant and mentor, and, you were the closet thing to a sister that I ever had. I miss you every day and even though you are gone, you will never be forgotten, for you live on in my heart and the hearts of all those who were lucky enough to have known you in this life. RIP my friend.

05.18.67 – 05.29.18

Acknowledgments

Thank you to my husband David, for his continued love and support throughout the years. I couldn't do this without you and I love you.

Chapter One

She couldn't breathe as her hands clutched the steering wheel and her stomach gave a little lurch. Trying desperately to focus on the car ahead of her, she tried not to think about what lie to either side of her. She hated this part of the highway and if she had had any choice she would not be driving it right now, but it was the only way to get to her destination. All she could see was what was in front of her as her mind tried to forget that on either side of her the bridge spanned the canyon and the raging river far below. For as long as she could remember she had been afraid of heights.

What seemed like an eternity but was only a matter of seconds she reached the other side and she breathed deeply, the worst of it was over. The road started to descend into the canyon, and soon the valley where the quaint little town of Silver Springs lay came into view. Looking ahead she contemplated what had brought her back to the town that she had not been too since she had been sixteen, and why she had just spent the last four days driving here from her home in Toronto. Or to be more precise, her old home in Toronto as Silver Springs was now going to be her new home, something she still could not believe was happening.

Driving past the sign that said 'Welcome to Silver Springs', she took in the view around her and noticed that not much had changed other than some new buildings and condos. It was the end of

June and the valley was a lush green with wildflowers blooming wherever they could find a place to grow. It was beautiful, but she personally couldn't see that since life in general had a very dark look to it right now, plus she preferred the big city. She still couldn't believe that she had given-up everything in the city to come live in this little hick town out in the middle of nowhere. But she had needed a change and to escape from recent events. Life had dealt her a cruel blow, but realistically it had been Frank who had dealt that blow to her, and to top it off her best friend Karla had just tragically passed away after her battle with cancer. Her heart tightened at the thought of her best friend and tears threatened to spill over, so she returned her thoughts to Frank to keep her mind off Karla.

Frank. Her fingers tightened, and her heart raced as she thought of what he had done. In one day he had turned her world upside down and left her with nothing. What she wouldn't give to be left alone with him for five minutes with no one else around. She smiled slightly at that thought and her fingers loosened on the wheel. It would never happen though, and she had accepted the fact that they had never meant to be together.

Pulling up to an old three-story Victorian, that had been freshly painted white, she took a deep breath to compose herself before getting out of the car. Nobody here knew about the problems she had gone through over the past six months except for her Grandma Susan and Grandpa Marty, and she wanted to keep it that way. In the eyes of everyone else, she was moving here for a fresh start and to remodel her grandparent's Inn.

She looked over the old building that was shaded by large oak trees and had a low hedge that ran along the front of the property. A white gate marked the entrance through the hedge and a path behind it lead up to the stairs and to the large veranda that wrapped around the front and side of the building. A sign post just outside the hedge and gate read, 'Welcome to The Inn at Silver Springs'. Looking around it brought back many memories of her childhood and she wished that she could go back to those carefree days. Taking one last big breath Alexis walked through the gate and towards her new life.

Jake sat behind the desk in his office and stared off into space. Marty and Susan's granddaughter was arriving today, and he wondered what she would be like. He had heard a lot about her over the years, but he had not seen her since they had been teenagers. He wondered if she would know who he was since they had never spent any time together. When he had last seen her, she had been sixteen and was just starting to develop. He had been seventeen at the time and of all the girls he had been interested in at the time, she had been the one he had never had the courage to approach. He wondered what she was like and if she still looked like the most recent photo that her grandparents had on their wall. Well he would find out soon since she was due to arrive anytime.

Alexis opened the large front door and entered a spacious front foyer and in the center of the room there was a round table holding a large vase of fresh flowers, the Receptionist desk just past

that. Much of the room was still decorated in a Victorian style and in
her opinion it needed to be updated. Walking around the table she
approached the empty desk and waited for someone to come help her.
She assumed they knew someone had arrived since a bell had chimed
when she had opened the front door. Turning her back to the desk she
looked around some more as she waited.

Jake heard the bell jingle letting the staff know that a guest
had arrived, he wondered if it was Alexis. Getting up from his desk
he left his office to go see to it as his receptionist Julie was on her
lunch break. His office was behind the receptionist's desk so when he
came out all he could see of his new guest was her back. Whoever
she was she was slim and had silky brown hair that was past her
shoulders. She was leaning against the desk and was not aware that
he was standing there, so he cleared his throat.

"Welcome to The Inn at Silver Spring's," he said cheerfully,
waiting for the woman to turn around.

Alexis turned at the sound of a deep male voice and she was
about to respond when she was penetrated by intense brown eyes that
looked like they could look right through you, down to your soul. She
shuddered a little at the thought as she took in the man's appearance.
He was well built with broad shoulders, had light brown hair and a
friendly smile on his face. He was dressed casually, and she
wondered who he was since he wasn't dressed as an employee would
be.

"Thank you," she responded after she finished looking him
over.

The first thing Jake had noticed when she had turned around was that she was average looking although some may consider her beautiful, but he had also noticed that there was a hard edge to her. There was also a look in her eyes that hinted to a woman who always got her way and that she had not been impressed with what she saw by the way she had just glanced over him. The way she held herself and her expensive clothes screamed that she was a city girl, something that had never appealed to him. 'You must be Alexis," he stated.

"Yes, that's me, how did you know that?"

"We've been expecting you, your grandparents told us that you would be arriving today."

"And who are you?" she asked in a haughty voice.

"I'm Jake." He didn't add anything else.

"Well Jake, do you know where my grandparents are?"

"They're around here somewhere, they've been anxious to see you since it's been so long." The last was said with a hint of disdain that didn't go unnoticed by Alexis.

She gave him a dismissive look and before she could reply two people came rushing into the foyer calling her name.

"Alexis! It's so good to see you, we've missed you so much," and elderly woman said giving her a big hug.

"I've missed you too Grandma," Alexis said hugging her back. "And you too Grandpa!"

Next, she was hugged by her waiting grandpa and Jake noticed that her demeanor softened as she spoke with the elderly couple, and he could see in her eyes that she loved them. He was amazed at her transformation from being a haughty city girl to a loving grandchild in a matter of seconds. He wasn't sure why she had been so cold to him but at least she hadn't been to her grandparents. He loved those two like they were part of his own family and he would have an issue with anyone who treated them unkindly.

The trio talked and laughed as if they had not been separated by years of absence and walked away down the hall towards the small dining room. Jake watched them leave then went back to his office to mull over the Wilson's granddaughter.   She was an enigma, one minute a woman with a hard edge to her and the next minute a soft caring granddaughter. Something had happened in the years since she had last been to Silver Springs because she had none of the characteristics of the young girl he remembered seeing when they had been teenagers.   Now she was here to live, and was supposed to renovate parts of The Inn, which meant that as the Manager he would have to work with her. He had a feeling he was in for a rough few months if she acted towards him the way she had a few moments ago. Jake sighed and wondered if he was up for the challenge.

Alexis sat at the small table in the dining room surrounded by her two favourite people in the world. Although she had not seen them in years and had not maintained a close relationship with them, she had missed them dearly. They had aged in her absence but otherwise they were the same lighthearted, carefree couple that she remembered them to be when she had been growing up and spent her summers here with them. Her grandma was telling her all about the rose garden that was her pride and joy, and of how she planned to add a few new bushes as well as a garden full of Alexis's favourite white lily's this summer. Her grandpa sat and listened and her with love shining in his eyes for his wife of almost fifty years. Yes, after all these years they were very much in love from what Alexis could see. She envied them, but her love and happiness for them out weighed that feeling.

"Alexis, did you hear me?" Alexis looked up realizing that she had been lost in her thoughts and had not heard her grandma speaking to her.

"I'm sorry, what was that Grandma?" she asked.

"I asked what you thought of Jake?" she responded.

"Jake? Oh, you mean that man at the front desk. What of him?"

"I was wondering what you thought of him. He's been working with us for almost ten years now and he's been a large part of the success of The Inn."

"Oh, really? I didn't know that, and I only spoke to him for a moment, so I can't really say what I think of him."

"You don't think he's handsome?"

"Grandma! What kind of question is that?"

"I was just curious."

Alexis didn't miss the look of amusement that her grandpa gave his wife. She couldn't believe that her grandma had asked her that ridiculous question, and as if she would be attracted to some small-town country boy who probably didn't know a thing about the world outside of Silver Springs. Besides, men were something she had absolutely no interest in right now.

"I guess he's okay if you're into that kind of look," Alexis finally answered since her grandma was patiently waiting for an answer.

"And what kind of look is that?"

Uncomfortable with the questions Alexis shifted in her chair and looked to her grandpa for help, but by the look he gave her she could see that he wasn't going to interfere in his wife's probing even if he did give her a pitying look.

"Umm, you know. An average everyday guy who dresses without a care in the world and probably leads a boring life and looks like he has no ambition to better himself."

"Alexis! I'm shocked that you would say that about a man that you don't even know. I know you've had your problems with men in the past, but I didn't think that you were that cold and unfeeling," Susan admonished. Disappointed with her grand-daughter she stood up to leave. "I have something I have to attend to," she said, then left without another word.

Alexis stared after her grandma and then looked to her grandpa confused. "What was all that about?"

Her grandpa looked at her for a long minute before answering her. "Your Grandmothers hurt because what you think about Jake means a lot to her. She's very close to him and to be honest, he's like a grandson to us. He's been with us for a long time and he's become a part of our family. And if I'm being completely honest young lady, he filled in the void that you left when you stopped visiting us."

"Grandpa, that's not fair," Alexis started to say before he cut her off.

"Yes, it is fair to say that. We don't know the real reason why you stopped coming to visit us in the summers, but it was hard for us, especially for your Grandmother. With your mother living so far away and you no longer coming to visit, we had no family left here. We've had Jake, and you, now that you're back and I must say it has not been the reunion your Grandmother was expecting." Getting up, Marty looked down at her before adding. "I must go see to your Grandmother and make sure she's okay. I suggest you take a long look at yourself and the way you look at the world, especially men. Just because one man treated you unkindly does not mean that all men are like that," saying that, he left without another word, leaving Alexis to stare at his retreating back in disbelief.

Alexis sat at her table for a long time, wondering what had just happened. In the space of twenty minutes she had happily reunited with her grandparents, apparently insulted a man she didn't know, upset her grandma and been talked down to by her grandpa. This was not turning out to be a good day for her. Maybe moving back here had not a good idea, but she had nowhere else to go. She needed her grandparents and the security they could provide her with the job of remodeling this place. Not knowing what to do, she got up and left the dining room through the patio doors and out into the expansive yard that lead down to a small lake.

With her head down, she wandered down the path and sat down on a bench under a large tree by the edge of the small lake. Looking out over the water, she didn't notice the beauty of her surroundings but only saw the darkness of what had become of her life. It seemed that no matter what she did things just kept going wrong for her and those closet to her left. Lost in her thoughts of feeling sorry for herself she didn't hear the footsteps on the pathway and someone stopping to stand in front of her.

"Are you lost?" Alexis finally heard a small voice ask her.

Looking up Alexis saw a small girl of perhaps eight years looking at her intently through large glasses and she had a curious look on her face. Her hair was pulled back into a ponytail and she wore loose jeans and a baggy sweatshirt. Her worn in running shoes scuffed at the ground as she waited for Alexis to answer her.

"No, I'm not lost. How could I possibly be lost out here, there's nowhere to go to get lost here, plus I know this place very well, even if I haven't been here in a long time," Alexis said to the little girl.

"Oh, okay. I was just wondering since you were sitting here staring off at nothing and looked lost."

Alexis stared at the little girl before saying, "did you mean lost as in thought when you asked me that?"

"Yes."

"Oh, that's was very perceptive of you because in truth I am feeling lost right now, in that sense," she added.

"I thought so, I seem to be able to tell how people are feeling. My father says it's a rare gift to have, especially at my age."

Alexis watched the girl shuffle her feet as she said this and wondered at how a child at such a young age could be so perceptive. She looked over the girl again and noticed that she had a small sprinkle of freckles on her cheeks and that for a girl she had a small measure of cuteness to her. Alexis did not have a lot of experience around children and was at a loss as to what to say to this little girl that was staring at her with large brown eyes, apparently waiting for her to say something to her.

"Umm, what's your name?" she finally asked.

"Becky."

"Hi Becky, my name is Alexis."

"I know."

Alexis was not expecting Becky to say that and looked at her sharply. "How do you know that's my name, we've never met before?"

"I've seen pictures of you before and have heard a lot about you," was all that Becky responded with.

"Pictures? Where could you have possibly seen pictures of me, let alone heard of me?"

"Grandma Susan talks about you all the time to me and my dad, and she has pictures of you in her office."

"Your dad? And who might your dad be?" Alexis asked, even more curious about Becky and why her grandma would be telling people about her.

"My dad's the Manager here at The Inn."

"The Manager and who might that be?"

Before Becky could answer her, the little girl heard her name being called and she started to run off. However she did stop to turn around briefly to shout out, "you're prettier than your pictures!" before racing off again and leaving Alexis stunned.

Chapter Two

Alexis made her way back into The Inn through a side door and wandered around, taking in all the changes her grandparents had made over the years. When her grandparents had originally bought the place thirty years ago, it had consisted of just the old Victorian home and the grounds it sat on. Since her last visit an addition had been added to the east side of the house that contained many of the guest rooms and the third floor of the house had been turned into a banquet hall. She also noticed that some of the furniture had been replaced but other than that everything else was as she remembered it.

Making her way back to the front foyer she stopped outside what she knew to be her grand-parents office and was about to knock on the partially opened door when she heard her grandma speaking.

"Oh Marty, I don't know what to do. She's not the little girl we remember. She seems so cold and distant when it comes to others. I was hoping that her coming here to live would help her forget what she's gone through, but obviously that man hurt her a lot more than we thought. I never expected her to have such a cold demeanor towards Jake," Alexis heard her grandma say.

"Give her time love. I'm sure she'll come around, and I'm sure she will warm up to Jake. I have yet to meet a woman who didn't like him," Marty replied.

"I know. Jake is a wonderful man and father. I just hope that things change because he deserves to have some happiness in his life."

"I agree and if I know you, you will get what you want in the end."

Alexis wondered what her grandpa meant by that last statement but brushed it aside as she knocked lightly on the door before entering.

"Grandma, Grandpa, can I talk to you for a moment?" Alexis asked stepping inside the office a few paces.

"Of course dear," Susan answered.

"I just wanted to say sorry to you both for earlier. I didn't mean to upset you and I hope you can forgive me."

"There's nothing to forgive Alexis, I shouldn't have sprung such a question on you. Especially right after you arrived, although I still think you were a little harsh in your assessment of a man you don't even know."

"I know Grandma, and I'm sorry. I'm sure he's a nice guy but you have to remember that my view of men is a little black right now, except for you Grandpa," she added quickly.

"Well that's nice to hear Lexi," Marty said warmly, using the nickname he had given her when she was younger.

Alexis stood there not knowing what else to say, so she looked around the office. A large bay window looked out over the gardens and the seat in the window was filled with pillows of bright colours. The rest of the room had wainscoting along the bottom, which was painted a soft white and the upper half of the walls were painted a pale green. Scenic pictures of the surrounding mountains graced the walls and one walled held numerous pictures of herself from the time she was a baby to last picture she had sent them last year when she had been in Paris. She was surprised to see so many pictures and the way they were displayed showed her growing up through the years. She was touched to see that her grandparents cherished all the pictures they had of her and she looked at them with a heavy heart.

These two-people loved her so much and she had failed to be a here for them for so many years now. This wall was all they had of her and she should have made more of an effort to be a part of their lives. She had let her cowardice keep her away after that last summer she had been here and that had not been fair to them. She vowed then and there that she would do everything in her power to make it up to them and to remake The Inn into everything they wanted.

"Grandpa. How come everyone refers to this place as The Inn instead of The Inn at Silver Springs?" Alexis asked curiously.

"Honestly, I don't know. I just remember one day Jake referring to it as The Inn and for some reason, and after that everyone started using that name. It just stuck and now nobody says the full name, even though that's what it says on the sign and everywhere else. Maybe I'll ask him why he did that someday since you've got me curious about it now," Marty said stroking his short white beard absently.

"Alexis, have you checked in yet?" Susan asked.

"No, not yet. I was about to when you two arrived at the desk. I guess I should go do that now. I left my car parked out front and I left everything I brought with me in there." Alexis answered heading to the door.

"I'll come with you. Marty, why don't you go move her car around to the back, that way it will be easier for her to unload."

"Yes Mam," he answered with a half grin, which made him look years younger.

Susan gave a little laugh and the three of them walked out of the office and into the front foyer. Marty took the keys from his grand-daughter to go move her car, and Susan went behind the desk to get a key and came back to take Alexis by her arm and lead her down a different hall. The two of them walked quietly as Susan lead them to the end of the new east wing and out the back door. Confused, she looked around and then to her grandma for an explanation.

"It's a surprise," was all that she got.

They walked down a gravel pathway and through the forest of towering pines. About fourty feet into the trees they emerged into a clearing which housed a large stone and log cabin, and what looked like a small guest cabin on the other side of a pond. It was like they had stepped into a hidden gem in the middle of the forest that no one knew about.

"Grandma, what is this place?" Alexis asked taking in everything at once.

"We bought this land about four years and built the cabins intending to rent them. But when we were finished Jake fell in love with the place and he bought the large cabin from us. The smaller one is empty right now and we thought that you might enjoy staying there instead of a small room in The Inn until you find your own place.

You'll also have your privacy and lots of space here. Of course, you have full access to all of the amenities at The Inn whenever you want," Susan added.

Alexis only half listened as she couldn't get past her grandma saying the Jake lived in the larger cabin. She was supposed to stay next door to the man she had just outright insulted to her grandparents. She wondered if she was being punished for her earlier behavior, but then dismissed that thought since it was obvious that these plans had been made before that happened. Before she could ask her grandma another question, the front door of the large cabin opened and a small girl in old sneakers and a ponytail came running down the front porch waving her arms.

"Grandma Susan, there you are! I've been waiting for you and I have something I want to show you," Becky said taking Susan's hand as soon as she reached them.

Susan smiled down fondly at the girl and Alexis recognized it as the same look she used to get when she was that age. A feeling of jealously started to arise but she pushed it back down and waited.

"And what is it that you have to show me missy?" Susan asked Becky.

"I can't tell you, you have to come see!" Becky answered pulling on her hand.

Laughing, Susan let the girl drag her away and Alexis noticed that they were heading in the direction of the small cabin instead of the large one. Curious, she followed along behind as the two chatted together and pointed at the different flowers along the path. A minute later they arrived at the small cabin and Becky let herself in and the other two followed.

The cabin was one large room with a stone fireplace, small kitchen and a door that must lead to a bathroom. Colourful pictures of wildflowers hung on the wall and a large flat screen television adorned one of them. In addition to that, there was a comfortable looking queen size bed, a sofa and coffee table and wooden table with chairs. It was beside the table that Becky was waiting for them.

"Aren't they pretty?" Becky asked pointing to the middle of the table. "I did that all by myself for Miss Alexis just now!"

In the center of the table was a ceramic vase holding a bunch of wildflowers that Becky must have picked from the surrounding area. The flowers were lopsided and the colours all clashed but it was obvious that Becky thought that it was pretty.

"That is the most beautiful bouquet of flowers that I have ever seen Becky. You did a wonderful job!" Susan said giving the girl a hug and giving Alexis a pointed look.

Alexis, not knowing what to say to the little girl who was looking at her with large eyes that reminded her of a puppy. She finally went with, "they sure brighten up the room."

Becky was obviously happy with this answer and smiled at her, showing that she had recently lost a tooth. Alexis couldn't help but smile back at that toothless grin and she saw her grandma give her a nod of approval. At least she hadn't screwed this up.

"Daddy said he will be back in a minute. He's gone to get something. You'll like my Daddy Miss Alexis, he's the best guy you'll ever meet and there's no one better than him." Becky said with a smile on her face for the dad she loved so much.

"I'm sure I will," Alexis answered, but she had a sinking feeling in her stomach as she put together the pieces of the day. She had a feeling she already knew who the dad was. She groaned inwardly as the realization hit her and she wished desperately that she could be anywhere but where she was now. Looking to her grandma, she could see that she had noticed that Alexis had figured it out, and in her eyes there was a hint of humor. It was obvious that she would get no support from there. Looking around again, she stopped when she saw the front door opening and she held her breath.

"Susan I've got Lexi's luggage here, but the rest of her stuff is still in the car. I wonder how she managed to fit that much in that tiny thing and drive it across the country?" Marty asked as he entered the small cabin with his hands full. He immediately put everything down in the first spot he could find for them.

"Grandpa, you didn't have to do that, I could have brought them in," Alexis said going over to him.

"Think nothing of it, I'm glad to help out my Lexi," he said with a fond smile.

"You're the best Grandpa," she said giving him a kiss on his cheek. "Where's my car parked so I can go get some more things out of it?"

"In the driveway out behind the large cabin."

"Thanks Grandpa, I'll be back in a minute," Alexis said as she headed towards the door, only to run face first into a solid wall of muscle.

Strong hands grabbed her arms to keep her from falling and she looked up into a pair of intense brown eyes that she could easily drown in. Alexis couldn't look away, something about those eyes captivated her and held her transfixed. She had noticed those eyes when she had met this man earlier today. She thought that they were the most beautiful eyes that she had ever seen and the watched her with interest.

"Jake, meet our granddaughter Alexis," Susan called out from behind her. "I don't believe you two have been properly introduced yet."

Jake looked at the woman he was holding and realized his assessment of her early had been off. She was beautiful and up close she smelled intoxicating. Dropping his hands from her arms he backed up a step and responded. "It's nice to meet you Alexis, your grandparents have told me all about you."

"I wish I could say the same, but it's nice to meet you too Jake," Alexis said, determined to not be rude this time to him.

"Lexi, Jake's our Manager and the best thing that has ever happened to The Inn. Without him we would never have accomplished all that we have here, and our success is all due to him," Susan said with pride and admiration on her face.

"Well I don't think I should get all the credit. You and Marty are The Inn and without you it wouldn't be what it is today," Jake said to Susan fondly.

"Oh Jake, you're such a delightful boy," she responded putting her hand to her chest.

Alexis watched the interaction between her grandmother and Jake and felt a pang of jealously. It was obvious that her grandma adored this man and it seemed that he could easily charm the old lady, but the look on his face clearly showed that he cared for her. Maybe he's not so bad and like other men she thought to herself, only time would tell.

"Daddy, Miss Alexis said she liked the flowers I picked for her!" Becky said loudly running towards him. Jake caught his daughter as she flew into his arms and he lifted her up easily. She hugged him and gave him a big smile.

"I'm glad she liked them Sweet-Pea, you did a wonderful job and it makes the room brighter," Jake said to his daughter as he gave her a kiss on the cheek.

"That's exactly what Miss Alexis said Daddy."

"Is that so?" he asked looking at Alexis.

"Yes Daddy. Isn't she pretty?"

Alexis cheeks flushed in embarrassment and she wished that she could hide. Her grandparents were watching them in amusement and it was obvious that Becky was waiting for her dad to answer,

"Yes Sweet-Pea, she is pretty, just like you," he finally answered.

Becky giggled at this and indicated that she wanted down. Once down she ran out the door and the adults were left alone in the now quiet room.

"Well, I guess I should go get the rest of Lexi's things," Marty said leaving.

"I'll help you," Susan called out as she followed her husband, leaving Alexis and Jake in an awkward silence.

After a moment Alexis was the first one to speak up. "Look Jake, I'm sorry if I was rude to you earlier today but I'm in a bad place right now and you didn't deserve for me to take it out on you. I hope you'll accept my apology," she added looking him squarely in the eye.

"Think nothing of it. It's forgotten, and I hope you and I can become friends since we are going to be working together a lot in the next couple of months," Jake replied.

"I would like that too and it just occurred to me that you're right. Since you're the Manager I guess we will be working together while The Inn is being renovated. I just hope that my grandparents like the plans that I started to come up with while looking around today. I haven't seen the place in many years and I needed to look around to see all the changes they've made before I could come up with some ideas for them."

"I'm sure that they will love anything that you do. They think very highly of you and are proud of the success that you've had with your Interior Design business. I'm actually looking forward to seeing what you have in mind for the place. But can I make one small suggestion?"

"Sure."

"When you're coming up with your designs I would suggest trying to keep to the character of the original house. It's been here a long time and it's a part of the Silver Springs history. It would be a shame to lose some of that."

"I'll keep that in mind and I actually agree with you. I've done a few older homes over the past few years and I've restored them to their original beauty with a touch of modern flair to them. I plan to do the same with The Inn. I loved this place when I was growing up and I want future generations to love coming here as well."

"You know what Alexis? You're not at all what I expected."

"Is that a good thing?"

"Yes, it is," Jake said as he smiled at her.

Alexis thought that Jake had a wonderful smile and was about to say something when Becky came running back into the cabin, followed by a large German Shepard. The dog immediately went up to Alexis and started sniffing her and she backed up a step.

"Don't worry, he won't hurt you. He's the best dog ever and he loves everyone," Becky said as she jumped up onto the bed and sat there watching her dog.

"What's his name?" Alexis asked unsure of the large dog that was still checking her out.

"Max. Grandpa Marty got him for me when I turned four because I wanted a puppy. I never knew he would get this big though, but I don't care. I love him, and he's my best friend."

Alexis looked down at the large dog who was now sitting at her feet looking up at her with large brown eyes. "What does he want," she asked no one in particular.

"He wants you to pet him silly," Becky said rolling her eyes.

Alexis looked to Jake, who looked like he was trying not to laugh and then back down at the dog. She slowly raised her hand to his head and gave him a quick pat on the head while saying, "good dog". Behind her she could hear Becky laughing and beside her Jake did likewise.

"Did we interrupt something?" Marty asked as he entered the small cabin carrying a box and a small suitcase.

"Not really," Jake said as he went over to Marty and took the box from him and placed it on the table.

"Ah, I see you've met Max Alexis," Marty said walking over to them to pet the large dog.

"Yes, although I have to admit that I'm not very comfortable around dogs," Alexis told her grandpa and backed up a few steps.

"Oh, he's harmless and he's one of the gentlest dogs you'll ever meet, no need to be afraid of him."

"If you say so Grandpa," Alexis said, still not sure of the big dog sitting in front of her.

"Marty, did you ask Alexis what her plans for dinner are yet?" Susan asked walking into the cabin carrying a large plant and a small orchid.

"No, I haven't had the chance to. Well Lexi, what would you like to do for dinner tonight?" Marty asked his granddaughter.

"Honestly Grandpa, I'm beat from the long drive here and I would like to just stay in for the night, relax and go to bed early," Alexis answered.

"But you must eat dear," Susan said worriedly.

"Don't worry Grandma, I'll get something from the restaurant and bring it back here. But I promise we will have lunch together tomorrow. I want to get some sleep tonight, so I can get up early and start planning the renovations for you."

"Oh, there's no rush on that. Take some time for yourself and get settled in first. You can start after the weekend, in fact, I insist on it."

"Don't argue with her Lexi, you know how insistent you grandma can be," Marty said chuckling.

"I wouldn't even think of it Gramps," Alexis responded using her old nickname for her grandpa. Maybe she should go back to calling him that she thought smiling.

Marty smiled at her endearment and headed towards the door with the others following him. "Call if you need anything," he said as they all filed out of the cabin.

Alexis didn't get to the chance to respond as the door was closed before she could say anything. Sighing she sat down on the sofa and closed her eyes. She was exhausted and wanted sleep, but she figured she should unpack her few belongings and go get something for dinner before she did that. The rest of her possessions, or more accurately what was left of her possessions after the sale of her house and large items, would be arriving next week with the moving company she had hired. What a nightmare that had been, and she was glad that it was all behind her now. But now she had to start from scratch in a town she barely knew and away from the big city that she loved. She hated small towns and now she had come to live in one. Not wanting to open her eyes and face her new life she sat there quietly and within a few minutes was asleep.

Chapter Three

Something cold was pressed against her face and Alexis tried to push it away with her hand, but it wouldn't go away. Opening her eyes, she found herself staring into the large brown eyes of Max, Becky's dog.

"What do you want, and how did you get in here?" she grumbled as she pushed herself up to get away from the dog. Even though she had been assured that he would not hurt her, she was still wary of the big dog. Her and dogs generally did not get along.

Sitting up, she looked around and saw that she must have fallen asleep for quite some time since it was starting to get dark out. Looking at her watch she saw that it was almost six and her stomach made a noise, reminding her that it was almost dinner time. She got up and flicked on the light switch on her way to the bed to get her cosmetic bag, she wanted to freshen up before she headed over to The Inn to find something to eat. Stopping at the foot of the bed she found Becky curled up in a ball sleeping under a small blanket. Now she knew how Max had gotten into her cabin.

Unsure of what to do, Alexis looked around contemplating if she should wake the little girl up or go find her father to deal with this. Making up her mind to go in search of Becky's father she turned to leave the cabin when a light knock came from the front door.

Walking over to it she opened it to find the man in question standing there looking handsome in the fading light.

At a loss for words all she was able to mumble to Jake was, "she's on the bed," and moved out of his way.

"I figured she was still here since she didn't come home a half hour ago," Jake replied as her entered the small cabin and went over to the bed where his daughter was sound asleep. "Sweet-Pea wake up, it's dinner time," Jake said giving the girl a gentle shake.

"Hmm, what's that Daddy?" Becky asked rubbing her eyes.

"It's dinner time. I sent you here half an hour ago to ask Alexis if she wanted to join us and you never came back."

"Oh, sorry about that Daddy. When I got here nobody answered so I let Max and me in and Miss Alexis was asleep on the sofa. I didn't want to wake her up, so I sat on her bed waiting for her to wake up, but I guess I fell asleep too."

"It's okay. Come on, let's go eat dinner, it's getting cold."

Becky hoped off the bed and went over to stand beside Alexis. "Will you please join me and my Daddy for dinner tonight? It would be so cool to have you there, it's been a long time since we've had company for dinner because Daddy never dates anyone."

"Becky!" Jake said with an embarrassed look on his face. "I don't think Alexis needs to know that."

"But it's true Daddy."

Alexis watched Jake and his daughter stare at each other not sure what to do. The fact that Jake never dated was interesting, but he wasn't her type, so it didn't much matter to her.

"I'm sorry Alexis, my daughter tends to be very blunt and to the point at times which can be exasperating," Jake sighed as he gave Alexis an embarrassed look.

"Don't worry about it. I actually like it when people are blunt and don't beat around the bush, it's makes life much simpler," Alexis answered with a small grin and a wink to Becky.

"See Daddy, she doesn't mind. Come on Miss Alexis, let's go for dinner," Becky said grabbing her hand and dragging her towards the door.

"Becky, you haven't given her a chance to answer if she wants to come for dinner yet," Jake called after his daughter.

"Of course she wants to come for dinner. We're much more fun than sitting in a restaurant by yourself, right Miss Alexis?" Becky said looking up at her with large eyes.

"If you say so," Alexis responded, following the girl out the door.

Alexis heard Jake let out a big sigh as he closed the door behind him and the three of them walked around the pond to the big cabin. Looking up at it in the fading light she saw that it truly was a beautiful home. She could only dream about owning a home like this now that she was broke because of her former business partner.

"You really do have a little piece of paradise here," Alexis said to Jake who was walking quietly beside her.

"Thanks. When Marty and Susan built the place, I fell in love with it and knew that this was what I wanted for Becky and myself. I was amazed that they let me buy it from them," Jake replied.

"I don't blame you, I would have been the same way. I envy you and Becky. It will be a long time before I can think of owning such a beautiful home again."

"Well you're always welcome to come and visit us anytime you want to. I'm sure Becky would like that especially since she's been doing nothing but talk about wanting to meet you and it seems like she already really likes you."

"She seems like a good kid and very spirited. I have to admit that I haven't had much experience with children though."

"Really, how come?"

Alexis thought about what her life had been like before Frank's betrayal and let out a small sigh before answering. "My life revolved around work and my social life. None of my friends or acquaintances had kids, only my best friend did, and as an Interior Designer I never met many kids through my work. But I was happy with my life and the way it was until things went bad for me."

Jake waited to see if she would say anything more knowing that something had happened to her to have made her move here and leave her life behind. He was curious as to what it was but had no intentions of asking her, especially since they had only just met and barely knew each other. He could probably ask Marty and Susan, but he wasn't sure if they would tell him or not. Realizing that Alexis wasn't going to say anymore he headed up the stairs to a large deck and led her through the door that Becky had left open.

Alexis followed Jake into the cabin and stepped into a large family room that overlooked the backyard and pond. High vaulted ceilings and beams spanned the room and a large stone fireplace dominated the one corner. The room was tastefully decorated, and Alexis was impressed with the care that had been taken with this room, as it could have easily been overdone. The living room flowed into a large kitchen and dining area that was separated by a long island, complete with bar stools.

Alexis made her way over to the table and found that it had been set for three people. It looked like Becky had been sure that she would come for dinner and she smiled at that. She liked this little girl even though she had only known her for a few hours. She reminded her of her best friend's daughter, and herself. A center piece of flowers that was almost identical to the one in her cabin graced the middle of the table and on the other side of the table Becky was already sitting down waiting for them.

"I hope you like chicken," Becky said from her spot at the table. "Daddy made a roasted herb chicken with potatoes, carrots and salad, he's the best cook I know!"

"I wouldn't say the best cook," Jake said modestly, as he placed a large platter on the table holding the chicken and vegetables that was for dinner.

"I'm sure it will be delicious," Alexis said with a wink to the little girl.

"You can sit there," Becky said pointing to the spot opposite of her. "That way you can sit beside Daddy."

"Okay, but first I should see if your dad needs any help."

"I'm good Alexis, please sit down," Jake answered as he put a bowl of salad on the table beside the other food. "Would you like some wine with dinner, I have a decent Chardonnay open?"

"That sounds wonderful, and thank you for inviting me for dinner, I wasn't really looking forward to having dinner by myself tonight."

"It's our pleasure. We know how much you mean to Marty and Susan and to be honest, I've been looking forward to meeting you too."

"So have I," piped in Becky.

"Yes you have Sweet-Pea," Jake said ruffling his daughter's hair affectionately.

Alexis didn't know how to respond to this, so she sat quietly while she watched Jake go and take a bottle of wine out of the wine fridge that was tucked into the island. She studied him as he moved around to get the wine glasses and couldn't help but notice that he had a spectacular physique and was graceful for a man of his size. Not wanting him to notice that she had been watching him, she turned her attention to Becky, who had been watching her watch her father. Blushing slightly, Alexis cleared her throat and tried to think of something to say to the girl, hoping that she didn't say the wrong thing.

An hour later found the three of them sitting outside around an open firepit watching the night sky. Dinner had been cozy, with the conversation mostly revolving around Becky, for which Alexis was grateful for. After they had cleaned up, Becky had pleaded with her father to have a fire before she had to get ready for bed and Jake had given in, having a hard time saying no to his daughter.

Alexis sat back in her chair and watched Jake point out the stars to Becky as she sat curled up on a chair close to her father. The two of them looked so comfortable together and she wondered if she would ever have that in her life. She was surprised with that thought and wondered where it had come from. Having children was something she had never thought would be part of her life as she had been content being a full-time career woman. Even when she had been engaged to Frank they had never discussed the possibility of having a family together. Alexis shook her head and thought it must be this clean mountain air that was making her brain become addled. Maybe it was time for her to turn in for the night before she started having even more strange thoughts.

"I think it's time for me to go to bed. It's been a long day and I'm exhausted from all the driving I've done this week," Alexis announced as she stood up and stretched her tired muscles.

"Already, but it's still early?" Becky said sadly getting up too.

"Yes, I'm sorry but I don't think I can stay awake much longer. But I will see you tomorrow, okay?"

"You promise?"

"Yes. I'll be at The Inn going over everything to see what all needs to be done in the morning, so I'm sure you will see me around."

"Cool! I'll make sure to come and find you after my swimming lessons."

"Sounds good," Alexis said then turned to Jake. "Thank you for dinner, I really appreciate it. It was nice to spend my first night here with you and Becky. It beat having to keep myself company."

"No problem," Jake said stuffing his hands in his pockets. "We're going to be neighbours so feel free to call on us anytime you want, or if you need anything, just ask."

"Thank you, I appreciate it. Night Jake, night Becky," Alexis called out as she started down the path that would take her the short distance to her cabin.

Although she did not turn around to look back at them, Alexis could feel Jake watching her and she wondered what he thought of her. She had been rude to him upon their first meeting, but she had apologized to him earlier. She hoped that they could be friends, it was something she was feeling short of these days. It was important that he like her since she knew how close her grandparents were to him, and to be honest, she had never met a man like him. Most men she knew were full of themselves and if she had treated any of them the way she had treated Jake earlier today, they would never have given her the time of day afterwards. Walking into her cabin she thought to herself that maybe moving out here would be good for her since she was already noticing some changes in herself after only one day. But she still missed the big city.

Jake watched Alexis walk to her cabin and disappear inside. She intrigued him in a way no other woman had before. Women from the city had always been a turn off for him as he had yet to meet one that didn't hold disdain for small towns and didn't know how to function without all the excitement of the big city. Whereas Jake loved his small home town and he couldn't imagine living anywhere else.

Then there was Alexis, who on the outside had the posh and sophisticated look of someone from the city and she had even been snobbish when they first met. Now that he had spent some time with her he could see that there was more to her than what he had originally thought. He sensed that deep down she was a good person and the way she treated his daughter proved that. Most people thought Becky could be a handful, always getting in the way and talking too much. But Alexis had been patient with her and had told her that she loved her floral arrangement even though he could see that see hadn't. She had lied to spare the girls feelings. For that act alone he had been willing to give her another chance and thought that by having her join them for dinner it would help to hopefully build a friendship between them. So far, his decision had seemed to work.

"You like her, don't you?" Becky said looking up at him and interrupting his thoughts.

"Hmm, what's that Sweat-Pea?" Jake asked his daughter.

"You like Miss Alexis, I can tell."

"And what makes you think that?"

"By the way you look at her Daddy. You're always watching her, and you smile more."

"Well she is very pretty, but not as pretty as my little girl!" he said smiling and picking her up. Although Becky was eight, he could still easily pick her up and he swung her around, eliciting small giggles out of her.

"Daddy put me down," she cried out between giggles.

"All right then, it's time to get ready for bed anyways."

"Awe, do I have to?"

"Yes Sweat Pea. Go on now, I'll be up in a few minutes to read to you, I just need to put the fire out."

"Okay Daddy," Becky said as she picked up her blanket and headed towards the house.

Jake watched his daughter for a minute then picked up the hose and started spraying the fire that was already burning down. When he was satisfied that it was out he put the hose away and collected the glasses from around the firepit and headed up to the house. He glanced one last time at the small cabin where Alexis was and saw that the lights were out already. Today had not turned out as he had expected it to when he had been waiting for Alexis to arrive, and she was far from what he had expected. Jake walked into the house wondering if that was a good or bad thing.

Alexis heard Becky giggling outside by the fire as she climbed into bed and thought that she had been lucky to meet them today. She had expected to come to the small town of Silver Springs and hate everything about it. She had used to love this place but after her experience the last time she was here as a teenager, she had vowed never to return.

Alexis rolled over onto her side as she thought back to that time so many years ago. She had been young and thought Silver Springs was a magical place where nothing bad could ever happen. But her fantasy had been shattered that last summer here and she had realized that she had been stupid and naïve. Something she vowed she would never be again. After that she had built a protective shield around herself and had never let anyone close to her. Even her beloved grandparents were pushed away until she rarely talked to them anymore. Her mother had tried desperately to find out why Alexis had changed but with little success. Life had passed by like this for her for many years until three years ago when she had met Frank.

When she had first met him, she had been completely enchanted by him. He was handsome, successful, and treated her like she was the only woman in the world. When he had asked her to marry him she had thought she had won the jackpot. Here was a man that had broken down all her barriers and whom she thought had loved her, but after their engagement things had slowly started to change in their relationship. He had become more distant, and she had thought she had done something to push him away, even though he had insisted that she hadn't and that everything would be fine. She had believed him and for two years she watched their relationship die until there was almost nothing left. And then it happened. Two months ago he changed her world forever and she wondered if she would ever recover from the devastation he had caused her?

Alexis wiped the tears from her cheeks and squeezed her eyes shut. It still hurt so much to think about it and she wanted desperately to forget what had happened. Breathing deeply she tried to push the image of his once handsome face out of her mind and tried desperately to think of anything else. It took her a long time to succeed in this and when she finally fell asleep she was emotionally drained and was haunted by Jakes handsome face in her dreams.

Chapter Four

Alexis woke the next day to the sound of birds chirping outside her window and sunlight streaming in. In her exhaustion last night she had forgotten to close the curtains, so she had a beautiful view of the pond outside. Thankfully no one was around, or they would have seen her getting up and walking around in her night shirt and panties. She closed the curtains then went to the small kitchen to see if anything had been stocked in it.

To her delight she found the makings for coffee and soon the aromatic scent of coffee beans filled the small cabin. While the coffee was brewing she quickly took a shower then threw on a worn pair of jeans and a comfortable t-shirt. She figured she might as well be comfortable while she looked around today making notes on what needed to be done and started planning out the new look for The Inn. She would ignore her grandma's suggestion to wait until the end of the weekend as she needed something to do. After finding a pair of sandals, Alexis poured herself a mug of coffee then took it outside to drink. She found a pair of chairs just outside her door and chose the closet one to sit down in. Sipping on her coffee, she stretched her legs out in front of her and enjoyed the quiet serenity that the clearing offered. It felt like she was the only one in world and that her previous problems did not exist here. She breathed in deeply and closed her eyes, wishing that she could stay like this forever. It had a been a very long time since she had felt this at peace with herself and the world.

Jake was watching the ground in front of him when he entered the clearing where his home stood. He was on his way back from The Inn to get Becky some sketching materials that she had insisted on having, so he had agreed to go get them for her. Since he worked all day, Becky spent her time at The Inn as well during her summer vacation. Although she did spend time out at the cabin with Susan occasionally and she did spend a lot of time at Sam's. But today she had insisted on staying close to him as she didn't want to miss the opportunity to see Alexis. Truth be told, he was looking forward to seeing her again too.

Entering the clearing he looked to the small cabin and saw Alexis sitting outside in a chair and it appeared that she was sleeping with a coffee in her left hand. He changed his course and headed towards her instead of his house. She was quite the sight in her worn-out jeans, t-shirt and her damp hair hanging down loosely around her face. This was not the same woman he had met yesterday at The Inn and he had to admit that he much preferred this version of her. She looked beautiful and like she belonged here.

Alexis heard someone walking up the path towards her and instinctively knew who it was before she even opened her eyes. She didn't know how she knew this, but she was correct in thinking it was Jake when she opened her eyes and saw him stop about five feet in front of her.

"Good morning Jake," Alexis said, looking up at him.

"Morning. It looks like you've made yourself at home here," Jake replied smiling down at her.

"Yes. It's so peaceful here. I feel like I could just stay here and never return to the outside world."

"I know how you feel. That's what I how every time I come home. It's like the world is shut out from this little clearing here in the middle of the woods. It's why I love it so much and why I wanted to buy the cabin from Marty and Susan."

"Well you are lucky to have this place. Maybe someday I will own something like this too. A place that I can call home and look forward to returning to every day." Alexis was surprised at how she had just opened up to Jake. For some reason she felt comfortable around him and speaking with him came naturally. Another thing that she hadn't been able to do for years. "I'm sorry, where are my manners, would you like to have some coffee? I have half a pot of fresh coffee inside."

"That sounds great," Jake replied as he headed to the door as Alexis started to get up. "No, sit here and enjoy your coffee. I know where everything is, so I'll be right back."

Alexis sat back down and did exactly that. A few minutes later, Jake was back outside, and he sat down in the chair beside her with his coffee. They sat there in a comfortable silence and watched the ducks that were swimming around the pond. Eventually Jake broke the silence by telling her about how Marty and Susan had purchased this piece of land years ago and their plans for it. Alexis listened to him and soon she was caught up in his story. Once he was done they chatted like they were old friends and they both lost track of the time as they enjoyed the beautiful morning.

Becky ran up the path from The Inn to her house to see what was taking her dad so long with her art supplies. He had been gone for almost an hour and he should have been back by now. Stopping to catch her breath before she reached the edge of the clearing she could faintly hear her dad talking to someone. Walking quietly she peered around the trees at the edge of the clearing and saw her dad sitting with Alexis talking away. Alexis was listening intently and would laugh occasionally. A big grin broke out on the little girls face as she backed up and ran back the way she had just come from.

Bursting into the office, Becky tried desperately to tell her Grandma Susan what she had just seen, but she was too out of breath to do so.

"Goodness gracious girl, what has gotten into you?" Susan asked as Becky collapsed into an arm chair.

"Daddy… he's… with…" Becky tried to say but still had not caught her breath.

"Take a big breath dear and then tell Grandma Susan what's got you so worked up about your dad."

Becky took a few long deep breaths before she tried to continue. "It's Daddy. He's over at Miss Alexis's cabin having coffee with her outside and they were laughing together. Oh Grandma Susan, I wish you could see him, he looks so happy. I haven't seen him like this in years."

"Really, you don't say?" Susan replied as a big smile spread across her face. "It looks like I was right in bringing Alexis out here, I knew he would be perfect for her. If anyone can help break down the barriers she's built around herself it will be him, and I still think they would be perfect for each other. I do believe that good things are about to happen here at The Inn again."

"What do you mean Grandma Susan?"

"Oh, let's just say that I think a new friendship has just been built and that it has the potential to become something wonderful."

Becky thought about what Grandma Susan had just said and then her eyes lit up as she figured out what she had meant by that. "You're hoping that they'll fall in love!" she cried out.

Susan tapped the end of her nose and smiled at Becky. She was a bright child and she was proud of her. "This is between us so don't go telling your dad what we just spoke of. This is between you and me, okay?"

"This will be our little secret Grandma Susan, and if I can do anything to help I will. I like Miss Alexis and I think she would make a great mom for me."

Susan smiled down at her and her heart warmed at those words. The poor dear had grown up without a mother since hers had walked out on her and Jake when she was just a baby. Jake had done an excellent job of raising her on his own and Marty and Susan had helped him as much as they could. For them, Jake and Becky were family and always would be. And, if things went the way she wanted it to then soon they would be marrying into the family.

"Does Grandpa Marty know about this?" Becky asked.

"Of course dear. There are no secrets between you Grandpa and me."

"Cool. Then we can all help get those two together." Becky said excitedly.

"Yes, I believe we all can," Susan responded laughing.

"What's so funny?" Marty asked entering the office to find his wife and Becky laughing.

"Grandma Susan just told me about how she wants my daddy and Miss Alexis to fall in love and I just asked her if we could all help her Grandpa Marty," Becky said getting up and going over to give him a hug.

Marty looked over to his wife shaking his head and tried not to laugh at the little girl's enthusiasm for Susan's plan. "And how are your plans going so far?"

Becky filled him in on what she had just told Grandma Susan and Marty couldn't help but grin. "It looks like our little Alexis doesn't have a heart of stone after all," he mused.

Jake looked at his watch and was surprised at how much time had passed by while sitting there with Alexis. Becky would be wondering what had happened to him. "I should really be going," he said to Alexis as he stood up. "Becky's waiting for me, I was supposed to be getting her some of her art supplies and bringing them back to The Inn for her. I'm surprised she hasn't come looking for me yet."

"Oh, I didn't realize that. I'm sorry I took up so much of your time Jake," Alexis replied getting up as well. "Here let me take that and I'll put it away for you," she said reaching for his mug.

As she took the mug, their fingers touched, and she felt a jolt and wondered at that. Taking the mug she backed up a step and looked at him in wonder. Had he felt that too?

Jake watched the play of emotions and questions running across Alexis's face and eyes after their hands had touched. By her reaction he assumed she had felt the same thing he had. There was something happening between the two of them that he didn't understand, and he was sure she didn't either.

"Umm, well, thank you. I best be going now, Becky's waiting," he said awkwardly. "Thank you for the coffee." With that he turned around and walked towards his cabin without looking back. He needed to distance himself from her right now. His body had reacted to her and he wasn't sure he was ready for something like that to happen.

Alexis watched Jake walk away and wondered why he had left so abruptly. Had he felt that jolt too and was running away? Or was he repulsed by what he had felt there. Sighing, she turned and went back into the cabin with the mugs and thought about the time she had just spent with him. She had enjoyed talking with him and it had felt good to have someone to talk to that wasn't only interested in talking about themselves. Jake was different from the other men she had known, but in a good way.

She was surprised with her attraction to him though because it was the furthest thing from what she wanted right now. A romantic attraction was not what she needed, what she needed was a friend. After Frank she had vowed to swear off men but here she was in Silver Springs for only two days and she was already attracted to someone. What was wrong with her? She decided that she would just have to make sure that they were never alone so her and Jake would just stay friends. Yes that should work, she thought as she picked up her notebook and tablet and left the cabin. Just don't touch him, her brain added silently.

Two hours later, Alexis had a general idea of what she wanted to do with The Inn regarding the décor and she had some suggestions for a few additions that she thought would help attract more cliental. She looked over her notes once more then headed for her grandparent's office where she knew they would be waiting for her. They were all going to head out for lunch at a small bistro in town to catch up and Alexis wanted to tell them her ideas.

She knocked on the office door before she entered and found not just her grandparents but Becky in there as well. The little girl was sitting at the large desk sketching pictures. Alexis stopped beside the desk and took a quick look at the papers scattered across its surface. She was taken back at just how detailed they all were. It was apparent that Becky was quite talented and had the potential to become a great artist. She picked up one that had caught her eye that was partially hidden under another drawing. She gasped in surprise as she looked at it, then looked down at Becky who had stopped drawing to watch her.

"I hope you like it?" Becky said shyly. "I was trying to do it from memory, but I think I could have done better."

Not knowing what to say at first, Alexis just stared at the picture. It was a sketch of her sitting under the tree by the lake with a faraway look on her face. Becky must have memorized this from when they first met yesterday then drawn it today. "It's perfect Becky. You couldn't have made it any better and I love it," Alexis said with a small catch in her voice.

"You can have it if you want."

"Really, are you sure you don't want to keep it?"

"I'm sure, I can always draw another one for myself."

"If she doesn't want it I'll take it," a masculine voice said from the doorway.

Alexis spun around to find Jake leaning against the doorframe and she wondered how long he had been standing there.

Becky giggled and said, "Daddy! I'll draw you another one, I want Miss Alexis to keep this one."

"Oh all right, but I'm going to hold you to that Sweat-Pea."

Alexis was blushing, being embarrassed from all this attention over a picture of her, and why would Jake want a picture of her? Unless she had been wrong in her assumption earlier when she had thought he had left because he had repulsed by the touch of her. Maybe, just maybe he did like her and that thought sent a shiver up her spine. She turned to see what her grandparents were doing and found them standing there watching her with big smiles on their faces.

Great, she thought, her grandparents are loving this and knowing them they would be happy if something happened between her and Jake. With that thought she narrowed her eyes and looked closer at them. Yes, she thought, there was something there and she was sure that she had just nailed it on the head. She looked back at Becky and saw the same smile on her face, then she turned to Jake. Watching him closely she saw that he was oblivious to this. Now she knew why her grandma had been so upset with her yesterday over her reaction to Jake. So, grandma was trying to play matchmaker was she. Well she was on to her, now she had to decide what she was going to do with this newfound knowledge.

Jake had been watching Alexis before he had made that bold announcement and he had been impressed with her and how she continued to show kindness to his daughter. She had been genuinely pleased with the picture and had told Becky so. It was that that had made him say that he had wanted the picture, which he knew had caught her off guard. Afterwards she had been looking at everyone, then her gaze had landed on him. It seemed as if she had been trying to read him as if she was looking for some kind of answer and he wondered what it could have been. It was obvious that there was something that the others knew and weren't telling her. It had him intrigued as to what it could be. He finally looked past her to his daughter who was also watching him.

"Hi Sweat-Pea, are you ready to go to Sam's?" he asked.

"Yes Daddy, just give me a minute to clean up and I'll be ready," Becky answered.

"Well Alexis, have you turned The Inn upside down with your inspection today?" Marty asked her.

"Not quite Gramps, I'm sure there is one or two plants that I didn't look under," she joked back.

"Well why not?"

"Oh Gramps, you never change," Alexis said smiling fondly at him.

"I try not to. So have you decided what you think we should do, and will I be broke afterwards?"

"Yes I've come up with some ideas and I think there will be just enough money left over to buy you some hair colouring for all those grey hairs that you're sporting now!"

"Oh dear," Susan said trying to stifle her mirth, whereas Becky and Jake did not hide their laughter.

"Why does everyone pick on me?" Marty tried to say with a straight face. That only sent them all into another bout of laughter.

"So what's this place we're going to for lunch?" Alexis asked when the laughter had died down.

"A small place called The Bistro that's on the main road in town. It's a newer place and everyone seems to like it. It's actually close to Sam's, so why don't you join us Jake after you drop off Becky," Susan said turning to him.

"Are you sure? I don't want to impose as I thought it was a family lunch," Jake answered.

"Nonsense Jake, you know you're family too and if we're going to discuss Alexis's plans as I know she will even though I told her not to start until Monday, then you should be there too since you are the Manager."

"Well okay if you insist."

"Of course I do dear. Now then, I need to go freshen up before lunch, so Jake you take Alexis with you since she doesn't know where The Bistro is, and we'll be there shortly. Come on Marty."

Before anyone could say anything, she breezed out of the office with Marty following his wife and giving Becky a small wink on his way by. Alexis saw that, and she knew that she had been correct when she thought that they were trying to play matchmaker.

"Come on Miss Alexis, you will love Sam's, it's one of my favourite places to go. You can check it out when Daddy drops me off," Becky said taking her hand and leading her out of the office.

Alexis looked to Jake as his daughter led her by him and Jake couldn't help but smile at the look on her face. It was priceless, and he wished he had a camera to capture the moment. He followed them out of the office and towards the front door. Once outside Becky continued to talk about everything while keeping a firm grip on Alexis's hand. It looked like she did not intend to let her have her hand back.

"Sam's is just the best place ever Miss Alexis. I've been going there every Saturday for the last two months," Jake heard Becky telling Alexis.

"So Sam's is a place then? I had thought that maybe it was a friend of yours," Alexis said looking down at the Becky.

"Well yes, Sam's is a place, but the owners name is Samantha and she's one of the nicest ladies you will ever meet. She lets me come to her store whenever I want to, and I spend hours there."

"What kind of place is Sam's?"

"You'll see, it's only a few blocks from here so we'll walk from here."

Apparently the two of them had forgotten about Jake so he trailed behind them and let them talk. It warmed his heart to see his daughter open up to Alexis the way she was. Becky had never had a mother in her life since her mother had left them when she was only eleven months old. Janice had not been cut out to be a mother and when she had had the opportunity to move to New York City with a man she barely knew she had jumped on the chance, leaving Becky with him. She had happily signed over full custody to him before she had left and since then has never acknowledged her daughter in any way."

It broke his heart that Becky had never known a mother's love and he was thankful to Marty and Susan for being the closest thing to Grandparents she would ever have. His parents had passed away shortly before Becky had been born and Janice's parents lived in Seattle and had no interest in their granddaughter. Now to see his little girl with Alexis made him reconsider his decision to not date. He had not wanted to date and bring women home to meet Becky, only to have her hopes raised that maybe one day one of them would become her step mom. In all honesty he had never met a woman in the last seven years that he had wanted to bring home to meet her and Becky had a hard time around women, possibly out of fear of being abandoned again. So he had stopped dating years ago and spent all his time with his daughter, worked hard and he hoped that one day he might meet someone that would be perfect for him and Becky.

Now there was Alexis. He had never seen his daughter take such a liking to a woman before, other than Susan and Samantha, and he wondered why. Although he could see there was more to this woman than what she let the world see. She was kind, had a great sense of humor and she had sat there and listened to him ramble on for an hour this morning. When he had felt that jolt when their hands touched this morning he had been shocked. It was a feeling he had not felt in a long time and maybe it was time he started thinking of the possibly that the woman walking in front of him right now might be the person he had been waiting for. He mused over that thought while he trailed after them on their way to Sam's.

Chapter Five

Sam's turned out to be a book store and a café. It was quite busy, and a few table and chairs had been set up outside for customers to sit at. It was a beautiful day out and most of the seats were occupied by people chatting away and taking advantage of the beautiful weather.

"Come on Miss Alexis, I want you to meet Samantha," Becky said tugging on her hand, trying to get her to go through the door that was propped open.

Becky led her into the store and she followed her having no choice since the little girl wouldn't let go of her hand. They passed a comfortable seating area with a fireplace and the counter for the Café. She was led past a few shelves of books and then stopped in front of a long counter.

"Samantha! I want you to meet my new friend," Becky said excitedly to the lady behind the counter that had her back to them.

The lady turned around and Alexis saw that she was a stunning brunet with friendly brown eyes that sparkled as she looked over the counter at Becky who was almost dancing in excitement.

"Well hello Becky, I've been waiting for you. And who is this new friend that you want me to meet?" Samantha asked glancing at Alexis.

"This is Miss Alexis. She's Grandma Susan and Grandpa Marty's granddaughter. She's living with us now," Becky said proudly.

Samantha lifted an eyebrow at that last statement and said, "really?"

Alexis nearly chocked on that last statement and cleared her throat before speaking. "Hi Samantha, it's nice to meet you. Becky speaks highly of you. I also want to clarify that I'm staying in the small cabin beside Becky's house."

"Ah, I thought as much. I think if someone was living with our towns most elusive bachelor we would all have known by now. It's nice to finally meet you. Becky has been doing nothing but talk about you moving out here for the last two weeks. Marty and Susan have also been talking nonstop to everyone about it as well. I feel like I already know you between those three."

Alexis was surprised at this and looked down at the little girl that was smiling up at her and was still holding her hand. "I'm flattered that everyone's been looking forward to me coming out. I have to say it's not something I'm used to."

"I think you will find things are a lot different here in Silver Springs than the big city. I've lived in a big city when I went to university and if I had to choose between the city and here, I would live here without a second thought."

"I've noticed the difference since getting here. It's nothing like I was expecting," Alexis said remembering what it had been like the last time she was here. Maybe things weren't so bad in a small town.

"Well I'm happy to have met you and any friend of Becky's is a friend of mine," Samantha said with a genuine smile on her face.

Alexis was touched by the sentiment and was not sure what to say.

"And who is this new friend of yours?" a deep masculine voice asked from behind her.

Alexis turned around to find herself staring at a broad chest. Looking up she saw a handsome man looking down at her with a curious look and she thought she would drown in his eyes that were a mix of brown and hazelnut. She was at a loss of words as she continued to stare at him.

"Brian, stop being so intimidating, you're making Alexis uncomfortable," Samantha said as she came around the counter to stand beside her. "Don't worry about him, he seems to have this effect on all women," she continued as she saw that Alexis was still staring at him. "Alexis, I would like you to meet my husband Brian Townsend. Don't worry, he's big but he's a giant teddy bear."

"Nice to meet you Alexis, I've heard many wonderful things about you," Brian said.

"Really? Is there anyone here that doesn't know me?" Alexis asked shaking her head and looking at Becky.

"I doubt it," Becky answered. "It's a small town."

"Don't worry about it. Here in Silver Springs not much is a secret because we're like one big family. We always look out for each other, and now that you are going to be living here if you ever need anything don't hesitate to ask," Brian said putting his arm around his wife.

"That right, anything, even if it's just to sit and talk over a coffee," Samantha added. "Plus you're already family because you're Marty and Susan's granddaughter, and everyone here loves that old couple and would do anything for them."

Alexis was stunned at the open friendliness of these two strangers and their love for her grandparents. She truly did not know how to react to all of this. It was new territory for her since the people she had always been around judged you first then decided if you were worthy of their time. But so far everyone she had met here was friendly and seemed genuine in their sincerity of friendship. Maybe things really had changed since she had last been here she thought again, or least she hoped so.

"Thank you, you don't know just how much that means to me," Alexis said with one of the first real smiles she had felt in years and with hope in her heart.

Jake had been standing off to the side while this exchange had been going on. He could see by Alexis's reaction that friendship was something that she must have been lacking in her life and he wondered why. She looked like she had been near tears at Samantha and Brian's offer of friendship and help, and he had had an overwhelming urge to give her a hug. She looked like she could use one. He knew that her life had not been going well lately but he didn't want to ask her about it until she was prepared to tell him herself. But for now he could give her his friendship and it looked like she desperately needed that. He felt that family and friends were something that she had not had in a very long time, and if he could help her he would. For now he would put his attraction to her to the side and just be the friend she needed. With that decided he walked over to where the rest of them were still talking.

"There you are Daddy, I was wondering where you were. Miss Alexis and I weren't walking that fast and shouldn't have lost you," Becky said.

"I was just checking something out in the next aisle over Sweat-Pea. Why did you miss me?" Jake asked tousling her hair.

"Daddy! How could I miss you, I just saw you ten minutes ago?" she answered rolling her eyes.

Jake looked a little embarrassed by his daughters comment and turned to Brian. "I haven't seen you in a while, what's new?"

Jake and Brian talked together while Becky took Alexis around the store to show her everything. Alexis was impressed by the store and how much business it was doing. It was the perfect place to come and buy a book and sit down with a hot or cold drink and relax. She wished there had been stores like this back where she came from but a place like this would have been snubbed by the circle of people she had chosen to be friends with. Although looking back at them now, she knew that had never really been her friends, they had been Franks friends. The only real friends she could truly say she had been her friend Karla, and an old high school friend she still kept in touch with, but Karla was gone now.

Looking around at the people in the store she saw a sea of smiling faces and everyone seemed so friendly. The city and this small town were like night and day and she thought Silver Springs might not be such a bad place anymore. Or maybe, just maybe it had always been like this and she had failed to see it because she had been blinded by the hatred from what had happened to her. The more she looked though, the more she was beginning to believe it was the latter. Becky calling her name broke into her thoughts and she turned to look where Becky was.

"Look Miss Alexis, this is where I stay for the afternoon when I come on Saturdays. Samantha made this area for me, isn't it beautiful?" She asked with a big smile.

Becky was sitting in a small tent in the corner of the room that was filled with pillows, and fairy lights were strung throughout it. She knelt to take a closer look and found a large golden retriever lying in the back of the tent watching her.

"Oh my, who is that?" Alexis asked.

"That's Baxter, he's Samantha's dog. He likes to sit in here with me while I read," she answered giving Baxter a scratch behind his ear.

"Is that what you do when you're here, read?"

"Yes. That's why I come here every Saturday. Samantha lets me read anything I want without having to buy it. Other than The Inn and Silver Lake, this is my favourite place to be, but I think I already told you that."

"Yes, I think you did, but I can see why you love it. I would have loved to have a place like this to go to when I was your age when I used to come and visit my grandparents."

"You used to come here when you were a kid"

"Yes, and it seems like so long ago since I was your age."

"You don't look that old."

"Why thank you Becky, I think that's one of the nicest things anyone has said to me in a very long time."

"Well it's truth, you don't look that old, right Daddy?"

"No, she doesn't Sweat-Pea," Alexis heard Jake answer from behind her.

Alexis felt herself flush at this and stood to find herself looking into Jakes handsome face. Not knowing what to say she looked around to see if Samantha and Brian were close by, but they were no where to be seen.

"Daddy, I think we embarrassed her," Becky said getting out of the tent.

"Perhaps we have, but it's the truth," he answered with a wink to his daughter. "Go find Samantha, she said a new book came in this week that she thought you would like to read. Alexis and I have to go, Susan and Marty will be waiting for us."

"Okay Daddy, have fun and I'll see you at dinner!" Becky said taking off to the back of the store.

Jake watched her go then turned to Alexis. "Ready?" he asked.

"Yes, I'm starving," she answered following him out of the store. She noticed a few of the female customers turn to watch Jake leave and a few gave her a curious glance. Once outside they turned to the left and followed the busy street.

"I hope Becky wasn't too much for you. She loves to talk, and I know some people have a hard time with that," Jake said the last part quietly.

"Oh no, she's a delight to be with. I've never known a child with that much energy and such a love for life. She reminds me of myself at that age"

"You don't know how happy I am to hear that. Becky's taking a liking to you and that's rare for her. Most women she won't talk to, except for Susan who is like a grandmother to her and Samantha who treats her like family. She's had very little female contact or role models to look up to. But with you, I've seen her open up more than she has to anyone before. That right there tells me that you are a rare kind of woman and I hope that you will continue to be a part of her life. I have a feeling you will be good for her and her for you."

"I'm flattered Jake and I'm not sure what to say. I'm very fond of Becky, even though I've just met her. There's something about her that I find endearing and it may be because of what I said before, she reminds me of myself at that age."

"I could see that. I overheard you telling her that you used to come here when you were younger. How come you stopped coming, if you don't mind me asking?"

Alexis stopped and faced him. "It's something I don't talk about, not even my grandparents know what happened that last summer I was here. I hope you don't think I'm a snob for not wanting to tell you, but it's something very personal that I don't like to share." Alexis explained, as she looked up at him and her eyes were pleaded with him not to ask anymore questions.

Jake saw this, and he could also see that what had happened had hurt her and it had caused her to stop visiting her grandparents.

He let it drop and smiled down at her trying to put her at ease. "It's okay, I understand, and you don't have to tell me. Besides, I don't think you're a snob, at least not since yesterday when we met," he added with a grin.

"Oh…you!" Alexis cried giving him a little shove.

"What, what did I say?" he asked laughing.

"Never mind, show me where we're going so I can eat."

"We're here," Jake said nodding to the storefront they were standing in front of.

Alexis turned to look and sure enough they were in front of The Bistro. But what got her attention though was her grandparents sitting at a window seat watching the two of them with knowing grins on their face. Alexis gave them a weak smile and waved to them. Looking at the expressions on their faces right now cemented the thought she had had earlier in their office. They wanted her and Jake to end up together. Well two could play this game and Alexis mentally thought about how she was going to go about this as her and Jake entered the restaurant.

An hour later found Alexis sitting back in her chair, sipping a cup of coffee while Marty and Susan went over some business issues with Jake. She had already told them the plans she had come up with for The Inn and was pleasantly surprised to find that all were in favour of the changes she wanted to make, including the new additions. It would cost a lot of money, but her grandpa had told her not to worry about it. Seeing as it was Saturday, Alexis would enjoy the rest of the weekend and start the work on Monday like her grandma had wanted her to. That gave her a day and a half to decide what she wanted to do with her free time. Maybe she would stop in at Sam's and buy a book to read. The thought of sitting out by the pond in front of her cabin to read sounded wonderful. Deciding that was what she was going to do, she turned her attention back to the conversation around the table.

"I need to get back to The Inn and finish some paper work before Kathy takes over for the night shift," Jake was saying as he put his empty coffee cup back on the table. "How much do I owe for my lunch?" he asked.

"Why nothing of course. We're the ones who invited you to lunch," Susan stated patting him on the arm.

"If you insist Susan. I learned a long time ago not to argue with you."

"Good decision Jake, I learned that almost fifty years ago when I married her," Marty joked.

"And your life was made easier by that wasn't it?" Susan shot back.

"Yes dear. Jake I'm going to tell you this once. When you do get married, remember the old saying, a happy wife means a happy life," Marty said grinning.

"Good advice Marty, I will remember that," Jake responded as he stood up.

"Oh Jake, would you walk Alexis back to The Inn? We have some business to take care of while we're here in town, so we won't be back for a while and Alexis would just get bored if she stayed with us," Susan said slyly.

"Sure, that is if Alexis wants to walk back me," he said looking to Alexis who was staring at her grandmother with a glare on her face.

"Of course she wants to, who wouldn't want to be walked home by the best-looking bachelor in town," Susan stated.

"I wouldn't say that," Jake started to say but was interrupted by Susan again.

"Nonsense, besides we can't have Alexis wandering around town by herself when she doesn't know the place anymore. Isn't that right Alexis?"

"Well I do know my way around some of the town still and The Inn is only a ten-minute walk from here. I'm sure I won't get lost Grandma," Alexis replied. "Besides, I wanted to stop back at Sam's to pick up a book I've been wanting read."

"Then Jake should definitely walk with you. Since you want to go to Sam's, he can check in on Becky while you're getting your book. That's settled then, off you two go and leave Marty and me to go our business."

Alexis gave her grandma a look that conveyed, 'I know what you are up to', before she got up to leave. Her grandpa gave her a look and shrugged his shoulders that told her there was nothing he could do to help her. Sighing she gave her grandma one last glare before exiting the restaurant behind Jake.

Once outside she let out a long breath and silently cursed her grandma. She liked Jake, but she didn't need her grandma purposely throwing them together. She wanted a friendship with him but with her grandma's meddling that may not happen. Sighing to herself she resolved to come up with an idea to stop her.

Jake had been watching Alexis since Susan had suggested that he walk her home. He had noticed a tenseness in her that he didn't understand. Did she not want to walk back with him? She had actually seemed up set with Susan for suggesting it. He wondered what was wrong and was unsure if he should ask Alexis what it was or leave it be, curiosity won out.

"Is there something wrong Alexis? You don't have to walk back with me if you don't want to, although I would like the company if you don't mind?" he asked her, silently hoping that she would agree to go with him.

"No, I don't mind walking with you, but it was very presumptuous of her to think that's what we should do. I forgot how bossy she can be sometimes," Alexis answered.

"I've noticed that too over the years, but I don't mind because she usually means well in what she's doing."

"Yes I know," Alexis sighed. "Come on, lets go to the bookstore and get that book I want, and I could use another coffee."

"Okay, sounds good to me."

The two of them walked slowly down the block and Jake pointed out the new stores as they passed by them. They passed the offices that Brian had recently purchased and soon they were entering Sam's again.

"Why don't you go find the book you want, and I'll get us some coffees and then check in on Becky," Brian said going to stand in line for the café.

"Okay, I'll come find you after I buy it," Alexis responded heading toward the fiction isles.

Alexis browsed through the books for a bit before finding the book that she wanted by her favourite author. She left the fiction isle and turned the corner to nearly collide with a stranger.

"Umph," she said looking up at the man she had just run into.

Steel grey eyes looked back at her with no hint of warmth in them. Something in the back of Alexis mind screamed that she knew who this was, and that she should leave, but she was having a hard time remembering who it was.

"Watch where you're going," the burly man said rudely. "Stupid tourist," he mumbled as he pushed past her.

Alexis froze as the man said those last few words. The voice and the way he had said it brought back memories, memories of her last summer here. Oh my God she thought, it's him. Panicking she put the book on top of the nearest shelf and ran out of the store with the need to be as far away from there as possible. On her way out the door she heard Jake calling her name, but she didn't stop. She couldn't breathe and had to get away, anywhere but here. She ran blindly as tears of fear started to blur her vision. She managed to make her way back to The Inn but instead of going in she went around back to the path that would lead her to her cabin.

Once she reached the path she ran as fast as she could and once in her cabin she slammed the door shut and locked it. She paced around the room unable to calm down and took big gulps of air since she was winded from her run. She was sure it was him. He had haunted her dreams for years after her last summer here and they had not been good ones. She finally flung herself on her bed and curled up into a tight ball as she relived the last time she had seen him. Tears ran down her face as she cried uncontrollably. He was the reason why she had never returned here, and he was the one who had shattered her young dreams.

Chapter Six

Jake watched Alexis run out the store as if there was a demon on her heels. Little did he know that that's exactly how Alexis was feeling.

"Daddy, what's wrong with Miss Alexis?" Becky asked coming up to him.

"I don't know Sweat-Pea, but I'll go find her and see if she's okay," Jake said picking up the two coffees that he had just paid for.

"Do you want me to come with you?"

"No, you should stay here with Samantha. I'm sure everything is okay."

"Okay Daddy. Oh Daddy, I saw her run into that awful man there before she left. Maybe he was mean to her," Becky added pointing to a man leaning against an aisle who was looking at the door that Alexis had just run out of.

Jake looked to the man that Becky was pointing to and swore under his breath. It was Ron Perkins, also known as 'Ron the pervert'. If Alexis had run into him it would explain part of why she had left in such a rush, but he wondered what he could have done to make her leave and ignore him when he called out her name. Ron then turned to him and gave him a lopsided grin that made Jake want to go punch the man in the face. He must have seen him calling Alexis name and realized that she had been here with him. Giving Ron a glare he left the store in search of Alexis. Since she was new here, there was only one place that she would have gone, her cabin.

He walked briskly down the street and made it back to The Inn in less time than it normally takes and headed back towards the cabins. He wasn't sure what he should say to her or if he should leave her alone for awhile before seeking her out. His instincts told him to go find her immediately, plus he wanted to go comfort her and make sure she was okay. Right now he was feeling an over whelming sense of protectiveness towards Alexis and he wasn't sure why.

You know why, his inner mind told him. It's because you like her, and she has been nothing but kind to your daughter. But mostly because you like her and because you know she needs someone right now, even if it's you. Jake knew his inner voice was right as he walked through the woods and out into the clearing where the cabins were.

Alexis's door was closed, and he saw no movement in the window as he walked closer. Stepping up to her cabin door, her knocked lightly as he juggled the now cool coffee cups in one hand. He waited a minute and then knocked again louder this time. Minutes passed before he heard her moving around in the cabin and then her footsteps came closer to the door.

Alexis was terrified, what if it was him she thought as he heard someone knocking on her door. When the knock came a second time, Alexis got up and picked up the heavy metal poker from the fireplace and walked towards the door.

"Who is it?" She called out with a trembling voice.

"It's Jake. I came by to make sure you were okay. You ran out and I was worried about you, so is Becky," Jake added.

Alexis sighed in relief as she opened the door and lowered the poker she was holing like a baseball bat. Jake eyed the poker and realized that whatever had happened was worse than he had realized.

"Expecting someone else?" he asked.

"What, no, I mean yes, I mean... I don't know," Alexis said breaking down into tears again.

Jake put the two coffees on the arm rest of the closest chair then pulled Alexis into his arms and held her as she cried. The sound of her sobs wrenched at his heart and he didn't know how he could help her, so he just kept holding her. Her stroked her soft silky hair and he rested his chin on the top of her head. Minutes passed, and they stayed this way until finally Alexis stepped back and wiped her tears away.

"I'm sorry," she mumbled. "I didn't mean to cry on you like that, look I've ruined your white shirt."

"It's okay, I have more. Beside you needed someone and I'm happy to be that person for you."

"You're a good guy Jake. There are not many people like you out there, or at least I have not had the privilege to have met one before you."

"Thank you Alexis, that means a lot to me to hear you say that. Now what else can you I do for you? I'm afraid our coffee is probably cold by now," he added looking at the forgotten drinks on the chair.

"I can't believe you brought those all the way out here," she said looking at them in surprise.

"Yeah, well, it seemed silly to leave them there after I had already paid for them. Not that I would have cared if I left them behind, I only wanted to make sure you were okay."

Alexis picked up the coffees and started walking towards his cabin. "Shut the door there will you, we need to go heat these up and you need to go get yourself a clean shirt. You have eyeliner all over it."

Jake shut the door and walked quickly to catch up to her. "Are you sure this is what you want to do? You don't want to lie down or anything?"

"No. I think the coffee will help me and I don't need lie down."

"Okay," Jake answered and walked beside her to his cabin. He unlocked the back door and let her enter before him.

They went to the kitchen where he pulled two mugs out of the cupboard and poured the coffees into them. Placing them in the microwave to heat, he told Alexis to have seat in the living room and that he would be right back. He went upstairs to change his shirt and then went back to the kitchen to get the coffees that were ready. Jake handed one to Alexis then sat down in the arm chair beside the sofa that she was sitting on.

They sipped their coffee in silence and stared out the large window at the pond below. Alexis sank back into the comfortable sofa and wished that life could be as simple as it was at this moment. It was a moment she wished could go on forever, but she knew she

owed Jake an explanation as to what had just happened. She just
didn't know how to go about doing that and how much she wanted to
tell him.

Jake watched her and could she that she was having an inner
battle with herself. He guessed that she was trying to determine
whether or not to tell him what happened

"Do you want to talk about it? If not I understand, especially
since you barely know me. But I have been told I'm a good listener
and I'm happy to help you in any way I can," Jake told Alexis.

"Thank you," Alexis replied after a moment of contemplation.
"I appreciate your kindness and I'm sorry I ran out of the store on you
like that. But I ran into someone from my past and it scared the hell
out of me, plus it brought back some bad memories that I have tried
for years to forget."

"Can I venture a guess as to that person being Ron Perkins?"

"Why yes it was, how did you know that?"

"Becky told me you bumped into him and then left right
after."

"She's a very observant girl."

"Yes, not much gets by Becky. So what made you leave after
seeing him, if you don't mind me asking."

Alexis stared out the window at nothing for a few moments
before finally answering him. "What I'm about to tell you, I've never
told anyone before except for my two best friends. I'm not sure why
I'm telling you this but for some reason I feel comfortable around you
and I know you will understand and not judge me, or at least I hope
not."

"I feel honoured that you would tell me this, but are you sure you don't want to tell your grandparents first?"

"No, I think if they ever found out it would devastate them, and I don't want to do that to them. It will be one secret that I will always keep from them I think."

"Okay, I respect you wishes, and I promise I won't judge you."

"Thank you. Okay, here goes. The last summer I was out here to visit I was sixteen years old. I had always loved coming here to visit my grandparents at The Inn and I thought Silver Springs was the best place to be. Over the summer I made a few friends and we would hang out together at the park or go down to Silver Lake to swim or go camping. It was the perfect summer until I met Ron. He was working a part time job here at The Inn for the summer, so I would run into him quite often," Alexis stopped to take a few deep breaths before she continued on.

"Ron was always pestering me and telling me I was ugly for a city girl. The way he teased me all the time eventually got tiring and I would go out of my way to avoid him when I knew he was working. My grandparents however thought that he was a sweet boy and asked why I never did anything with him. For one he was always mean to me and two he was three years older than me. I told them that he wasn't the kind of person I wanted to hang around with, but they didn't understand why.

"The last week I was here I was out hiking on the paths out behind The Inn that wind through the forest and end up at the river. I was by myself when Ron appeared out of nowhere and blocked my way. I asked him to let me by, but he refused and called me an ugly city girl again, then said that he had heard all city girls were easy.

"It was then that I realized that he had been picking on me because I wouldn't give him the time of day and he wanted something from me, something I wasn't willing to give him. I tried to push my way past him, but he was too strong, he shoved me, and I fell. Before I knew it, he was on top of me," Alexis stopped there as she tried to choke back the tears that had come again. After gaining some control she managed to finish her story.

"He tried to rip my shirt open as I struggled to try and get him off me. He was grinning down at me as he was doing this, and he said, 'you're such a tease, you know what I want, and I know that all city girls are sluts so just give it up'. It was then that I heard laughter and I looked to see that there were two more guys there now. Two of them I had thought had been my friends since I had been hanging out with them and their friends all summer. I was so scared of what was happening and the fact that they were watching and laughing meant that they were in on this too. They were planning to gang rape me and I was still a virgin." Alexis had to stop here because she could no longer hold back the tears and started crying uncontrollably. Her whole body shook, and she hung her head in despair.

Strong arms surrounded her and held her gently. Alexis leaned into those arms and held on. She was an utter wreck and having to say those things out loud brought all the pain back as if it had happened yesterday. Jake continued to hold her, and his heart broke at the thought of what she had gone through, and on her own. His heart wanted to go find Ron and pummel him into the ground, again, but his brain told him not to act rashly and stay there with Alexis. He listened to the latter and stayed where he was.

He leaned back into the sofa and continued to hold her. Alexis needed a friend right now and he would give her anything she needed. After hearing her story he could now understand why she had never returned before yesterday and why she had such a low opinion of small towns. He promised himself that if he ever got a chance, he would deal with Ron, especially since this was something that Ron had been known to do in the past but had never got in trouble for until a few years later. Hence his nickname, Ron the pervert.

Alexis slowly started to regain control of herself and her crying lessened to the odd tear being shed. She sniffled and imagined that she looked a wreck right now. Here she was crying on Jake again.

"I'm sorry, I seemed to have ruined another one of your shirts Jake," she said wiping his damp shirt.

"It's okay, it's just a shirt," he said while still holding her.

"That's twice I've done that in the last half hour and I seem to be saying I'm sorry a lot too."

"I don't mind. If this is what it takes to help ease the pain you're going through right now, then it was worth it. I'll let you ruin all of my shirts if it will make you feel better."

"Thank you, Jake, I'm lucky to have made a friend like you."

"And I'm lucky to have met you. I will always be here if you need anything or a shirt to cry on," he said the last with a small grin.

Alexis smiled and thought she was truly lucky to have met him yesterday and formed a friendship with him. Although he was still virtually a stranger to her, she felt comfortable with him and she felt like she had known him a lot longer than just over twenty-four hours. She also felt content to be leaning on him and having him still holding her. It felt right, but she shifted to sit up anyways. She didn't want to abuse his friendship and to be honest, it had felt so good that she was starting to feel a warmth surging through her body that was centering towards her lower regions. This was not something she wanted to deal with just now, so she thought it safer to put a little distance between them.

She got up off the sofa and went to stand by the large picture window and stared off into the forest beyond. Somewhere out in that direction is where she had lost her trust and faith in men for a very long time. Then when she had thought she could trust a man again he had stomped all over her heart. And now here was Jake. He was everything a woman would want in a man, kind, caring, a family man and good looking. But all she wanted was to be friends with him. The fiasco with Frank was still too fresh and she was not ready to trust another man with her heart, even if the man sitting on the sofa behind her was next to perfect. She sighed and continued to stare at the forest some more.

Jake let her go, sensing that she needed to put some space between them. He had felt a familiar warmth spreading through his body with her that close to him. She had fit perfectly into his arms and she had smelled intoxicating. It was a good thing that she had moved because if she had sat there for much longer his attraction to her would have become apparent. With what she had just shared with him, he didn't think that would be a good idea.

So he let her stand there by herself for a while to give her some space and after about five minutes he got up to go stand beside her, his body now cooled down.

"Alexis, you don't have to answer this if you don't want to, but did Ron…?"

"No," Alexis answered before he could finish his question and she turned to him. "He never got the chance to because we heard someone coming down the path which distracted him. I was able to knee him in the groin while he was distracted which got him to let go of me. I then punched him in the nose while he was holding himself and I was able to get up and run away before the other boys knew what had happened and were able to react. I ran as fast as I could and all I could hear was him screaming at me and calling me a stupid city bitch, and that he would get me for this and if I told anyone he would kill me. By the time I made it back to The Inn my clothes were ruined, and I had completely broken down.

"When my grandparents saw me they tried to find out what had happened but all I would tell them was that I had fallen down a small hill on my hike and that I would be okay. I was too terrified to tell them what had happened. I was also scared of what Ron would do to them if he found out I had told them.

"So I hid in my room for the rest of the day and pleaded with my grandparents to let me go home early because I wasn't feeling well. They eventually gave in and took me to Calgary the next day to fly home. I haven't been here since then, so when I ran into Ron today all those fears came rushing back and I felt the same as I had that day so many years ago," Alexis finished.

Jake was both proud of how she had been able to fight off Ron that day and sad for the girl who had been traumatized that day and almost lost her innocence. Now more than ever he wanted to find Ron and tear him to pieces. If he ever ran into him again Ron had better start running like Alexis had that day because Jake felt like he would kill the man for what he had done to her.

"You are by far one of the strongest women I have ever known Alexis. To have to have gone through that and then live with it on your own takes a lot of strength and courage," Jake said taking her hand and giving it a gentle squeeze.

"Thank you, Jake. Now that I've had someone else to tell my story to I feel better. To know that you listened and didn't judge me for what happened shows your character as a man and I am proud to call you my friend. I will never be able to see you as one of the bad guys like I have with most of the men in my life," Alexis responded squeezing his hand back.

They stood there and stared into each other's eyes for a long time before they both looked away. It was Jake who finally let go of her hand and walked away.

"I don't know about you, but I think we could both use something to drink that's a lot stronger than those two warm coffees," he called out over his shoulder as he headed for the kitchen.

"I agree," Alexis said picking up the coffees that had gone cold again. "What did you have in mind?"

"What's your preference? I have wine, beer or hard liquor if you're in the mood for that."

"Actually a cold beer sounds perfect right about now."

"Two beers coming right up then." Jake grabbed two cold beers out of the fridge and twisted the tops off them before handing one to Alexis. "To Alexis, the strongest woman I know," he said as he clinked her bottle with his.

She smiled back at him before taking a drink and she savoured the coolness of it as it slid down her parched throat. The beer was delicious and hit the spot, it was exactly what she had needed after all the emotional turmoil she had just gone through. Jake had moved around the island and she followed him as he went out onto the back porch to sit on the outdoor sofa. They relaxed as they drank their beer in silence and Alexis thought to herself that if she was ever going to let herself fall for a guy again, Jake would be the perfect man to do that with.

Chapter Seven

Alexis woke up to the sound of voices and she felt a little disoriented, not sure of where she was. The last thing she remembered was sitting outside with Jake drinking a beer. She opened her eyes and found that she was laying down on the sofa outside with a light blanket covering her. She sat up and swung her legs off the sofa, only to have them land on something soft and warm. She looked down and found Max lying down in front of her, she had just put her feet on top of his back.

"Hi Max, have you been here the whole time?" Alexis asked him and scratched him behind his ear.

"He's been watching over you the whole time you've been asleep," Jake answered coming out of the house with a fresh bowl of water for Max. "Dogs are supposed to be able to sense your feelings and I think he sensed your distress and decided to stay by you and protect you."

Surprised at this news, Alexis looked down to Max again with a whole new appreciation for him. She had never been a huge dog lover, but he was changing her thinking. "Thank you Max," she said giving him another scratch behind his ear.

"If you keep doing that he'll never leave your side, he loves having his ears scratched."

Alexis stood up and stretched and Jake admired her figure as she was doing that. She could still hear voices coming from within the house and she wondered who was here. She didn't have to wonder for long because Becky came running out of the house and launched herself at Alexis giving her a big hug.

"Oh Miss Alexis, I was so worried about you. You went running out of the store without Daddy and I knew something was wrong. I wanted to come and see you, but Daddy told me he would go check on you. Are you okay now? I saw that mean man Ron run into you. I don't like him, and I don't think anyone else does either. There's something weird about him," Becky added.

Alexis was both shocked and humbled by the little girls worry over her and she hugged her back. "I'm fine now Becky. You're Daddy and I had a long talk and he helped me to feel better. I'm sorry I worried you," Alexis said as the girl hugged her tighter.

"I'm glad Miss Alexis, I don't want you to be sad. And I'm sure if that bad man Ron said or did something to you that my Daddy will take care of him for you."

Alexis was taken back by that last statement and she looked over the girl's head at Jake who was not alone anymore. Samantha and Brian were standing by his side now watching them. Becky let go of her then and turned to see what she was looking at.

"Everything's okay now Samantha," Becky called out. "Daddy talked to her and he's going to take care of everything, so it doesn't happen again."

"Becky," Jake started to say but was cut off by his daughter.

"You are going to help her right Daddy. You can't let Ron be mean to her again. I'm sure Brian would be happy to help you too, right Brain?" she said with a hopeful look at them both.

"Umm, I guess so Becky, but what exactly am I supposed to be helping your dad with?" Brian asked.

"You and Daddy need to go see Ron and make sure he doesn't hurt Miss Alexis again. If you won't then I will. I don't like him, and I will happily kick him in the leg and tell him to leave our Miss Alexis alone!"

"Becky!" Alexis said, shocked again at her outburst. "I'm sure everything is going to be okay and I appreciate your wanting to help but please promise me you won't go anywhere near that man."

"But Miss Alexis, he…"

"No Becky, promise me you won't. You're right when you said he's a bad man and I don't want you anywhere near him. Now promise me you won't go and do anything foolish."

"Alright," Becky said looking down at the deck. "I just want to help you. I like you and I don't want anything to happen to you."

"I know Becky, and I appreciate that. You don't know how lucky I am to have a friend like you." With those words Becky looked up the gave her a big hug again before she ran back into the house.

Alexis watched her go then turned to the others who had stood by quietly while watching Becky.

"Well, I must say, Becky sure had taken to you Alexis," Samantha said breaking the silence. "I've never known her to open up to anyone this much or be this protective."

"And I'm honoured that she feels that way with me. I have to admit that I don't have much experience with children, but I have grown quite fond of Becky. As I've said before, she reminds me of a younger me," Alexis said wistfully.

"Well I'm glad she has you in her life," Samantha said smiling at her.

"I'm happy to be a part of her life too, she has shown me in only two days how to open up and enjoy what there is around me. I'll admit that I can be a hard person to be around but that had to do with trust issues from my past. But being here has helped me realize that the world is not as bad as I had once thought it was, or that not all people are out to hurt you. Just look at the kindness that you, Brian and Jake have shown me, and you barely know me. In all the years that I lived in the city, I never met anyone as nice as you three. I am truly grateful to have all of you in my life and I hope to build strong friendships with each of you," Alexis said meaning every word of what she had just said.

"And we are happy to have met you as well Alexis, I believe that we will all get along great. Plus we already know so much about you, your grandparents talk about you all the time and we can tell that they love you very much."

"Is there anyone in this town that my grandparents haven't talked to me about me?" Alexis groaned. Everyone laughed at that and it helped lighten to mood for a moment.

"So what's this about Ron?" Brian asked. "Did he hurt you or say something he shouldn't have to you in the store today?"

Alexis looked to Jake wondering if he would say anything. He looked back at her and she could tell by the look in his eyes that he wasn't going to say anything. Sighing Alexis figured that maybe it was time to let people know what had happened to her all those years ago. Telling Jake earlier had felt refreshing and it felt like a great weight had been lifted off her by not having to hide her past experiences anymore.

Still looking at Jake she finally spoke up. "Go ahead Jake, they should know, especially since it will be hard to avoid Ron in a town this small and I would rather they knew the truth instead of whatever lies he may tell everyone."

"Are you sure?" Jake asked her.

"Yes, I'm sure."

"Why do I have a feeling we should be sitting for this?" Samantha asked as she sat down on the sofa and motioned for Alexis to sit beside her. Jake and Brian sat down in the matching chairs apposite the women.

"Alexis just told me her story about an encounter with Ron and some of his friends when she was sixteen, and I have a feeling the two of you are not going to be surprised by what I tell you," Jake said giving Samantha and Brian a knowing look.

Alexis was surprised by his statement and looked at him sharply.

"That bastard!" Brian yelled shooting up out of his chair.

"Is there something I don't know?" Alexis asked, looking at the looks of anger on the men's faces and sadness on Samantha's.

"You're not the only person Ron has done this to Alexis," Samantha said taking her hand. "He's was accused of doing the same thing to a few other girls when he was younger. When he was twenty-two he was charged with beating up his girlfriend and raping her friend. He spent time in jail but got out early on good behavior. He's only been back in town for about five months now."

"That's five months too long," Jake grumbled.

"Agreed," Brian said. "Is there no way to make him leave town? I would prefer to not have a man like that living in the town that I plan on raising our children in."

"I'm not sure, but if anyone would know it would be your lawyer, Mr. Webber," Samantha suggested.

"Good idea hon, I'll give him a call first thing Monday morning."

"Have you been keeping this a secret all these years Alexis?" Samantha asked.

"Yes," Alexis answered overwhelmed by all of this.

"Might I venture to guess that this is the reason why you never came back after that summer?"

"Yes."

"I see, and I gather your grandparents don't know since they've always wondered why you stopped visiting them?"

"No, they don't. It would break their hearts to know what happened to me."

"I don't know Alexis. I've known you're grandparents my whole life and they are two of the strongest people I've ever known. I think you'd be surprised at what their reaction would have been."

"I think I'm beginning to see that now. Just by opening up to Jake today and now you, I've realized that this is not something I needed to keep secret because I was worried about what people would think of me and what Ron would do."

"Well you have all of us to help you now and we will never let Ron hurt you again, right guys?"

"Damn right," Jake said, and Brian nodded too.

"You guys are the best. I don't know what I did to deserve meeting all of you and having you as part of my life now," Alexis stated while wiping away a tear of happiness away as Samantha gave her a hug.

What had been a horrible afternoon for her had turned into a pleasant surprise and she now knew that moving here had not been a mistake. The four of them sat around and talked afterwards and told stories. Alexis learned that Samantha and Brian were older than her and Jake and that they had both been born in Silver Springs. Brian had moved away for many years though and had only just returned this year when his younger brother had passed away. He and Samantha had rekindled what they had once had, and they had only just recently married. Alexis felt comfortable talking with all of them and felt like she belonged here.

"Daddy, are you guys almost done with grown up talk? I'm starving, and Max is eying the steaks on the counter!" Becky asked from the doorway.

"Yes we're done!" Jake called back standing up.

"I guess I should get going too," Alexis said getting up as well. "I should go see about finding something for dinner too."

"You don't have to leave Miss Alexis, I want you to stay for dinner too. Brian and Samantha are staying for a barbeque and we have enough food for everyone, right Daddy?"

"We sure do Sweat -Pea, that is if Alexis wants to stay," Jake answered looking at Alexis.

"Please stay, we can roast marshmallows around the fire afterwards," Becky pleaded.

Alexis took one look at the girls large pleading eyes and laughed. "How could I say no to a face like that?"

"Yes! I knew you would stay, now I will have my six favourite people in the world here tonight. This is going to be so much fun!" Becky said excitedly before racing across the deck and down the path.

"Six people?" Alexis asked.

Jake nodded his head in the direction that Becky had just run off to and Alexis saw her grandparents coming up the path from The Inn.

"Oh," was all that Alexis said upon seeing her grandparents being met by an excited Becky.

"Are you okay?" Jake asked as he came to stand by her.

"What? Oh yes, I'm fine. It's just that I'm sure word has spread, and they'll be wondering what happened today and I'm not sure if I'm ready to tell them yet."

"I think you should tell them, as Samantha said earlier, they're stronger than you think they are. I've known them my whole life too and I agree with her."

"I guess you're right, the sooner the better."

"If you want I'll stay with you if you want me too."

"I appreciate the offer Jake, but I think I should do this on my own," Alexis replied giving him a warm smile before she went down the steps and walked toward her grandparents.

Jake watched her go and realized in that moment just how much he admired her and was happy that she was a part of his life now too.

Jake was in the kitchen preparing the steaks when he stopped to look out the window at the three people talking down by the pond. Alexis, Marty and Susan were standing close together and it was at that moment that he saw Susan's hand go to her mouth in shock and then hug her granddaughter. Even from this distance he could tell Alexis was crying and he wished that he could be there for her, but for now she needed to be with them alone. He would be there for her later if she needed him.

"You like her don't you?" Brian asked sitting on a barstool in front of him.

"What do you mean?" Jake asked as he finished seasoning the last steak and pushed the platter to the side.

"I can see it in the way you watch her that you've taken a liking to Alexis. I can also tell that you're itching to go down there and be there for her."

"Am I really that transparent?"

"Yes you are. I know we've only recently become good friends, but even a stranger could see it."

"Well I doubt that anything will happen since she's made it clear that she's just looking to be friends, and I'm fine with that. Especially since we're going to be working together over the next couple of months on the new renovations to The Inn. Besides, I don't want Becky to get her hopes up. I know she likes Alexis and I'm sure she's going to be asking about us soon."

Brian looked at his friend for a moment before saying anything. "But you like her and want it to be more than a friendship, even if you say you don't."

Jake sighed and grabbed two beers out of the fridge and walked around the island to sit beside Brian. "Yes, I'll admit that I do, but what can I do when that's not what she's looking for. Especially after learning about her past today, plus I have a feeling that she just came out of a bad relationship."

"Then be her friend, and see where it goes, there's nothing saying you can't lay on your charms over time. Let her get to know you and then maybe when's she's ready ask her out. Who knows, she might change her mind about how she sees you in the near future if you're lucky."

"I guess I could do that. I've always had my aversion to city women, but there's something different about her. She's someone I could see falling in love with and wanting to spend my life with. I know that sounds crazy after only knowing her for two days but like I said she's different, she's special. Plus look had how great she is with Becky, and Becky adores her."

"It's not crazy my friend and I suggest that you follow what your heart is telling you. Life is too short, so make the best of it and I think that young lady out there is what you've been looking for. Although you will break a lot of hearts in town if you cease to be Silver Springs most eligible bachelor!" Brian joked as he clinked Jakes beer bottle with his.

Jake laughed and the two of them sat there looking out the window at the woman that Jake was falling for.

Alexis wiped her tears away realized that Samantha and Jake had both been right in their perception of her grandparents. They had taken the news a lot better than she had thought they would and had been sympathetic and supportive. Alexis had also learned that they had had their suspicions that Ran had been the reason why she had left because of some off handed remarks he had made about her. They had also had to fire him a few weeks after she had left for inappropriate behavior towards their female employees.

Alexis felt ashamed and guilty for what she had put them through over the years and promised them that it would never happen again. They all hugged each other one last time before heading towards the main cabin where everyone was waiting for them.

Dinner turned out to be a lively event and Becky made sure that Alexis never had a moment to be sad or think about what had happened that day. For the first time since that summer she had been sixteen, Alexis truly felt like she was part of a group of friends that were real, and that she would hold this moment dear for the rest of her life.

It was a night to be remembered and by the end of it she was wondering if maybe she was wrong in thinking that she only wanted Jake as a friend. He had been the most supportive of all of them and had stuck close by her all night to make sure she was okay. When they had retired to the firepit to roast marshmallows, he has sat beside her and by the end of the night he was holding her hand, much to Becky and Susan's delight!

Chapter Eight

Alexis woke the next morning feeling better than she had in a long time. For the first time in months she did not dread the prospect of having to get up and face the world. She stretched and contemplated on just staying in bed for another hour. It had been a long time since she allowed herself that luxury. Rolling over she pulled the covers up intended to do just that. She fell asleep and did not wake up again for another hour.

When she did finally get up she took her time and showered then opened up her tablet to check out what was going on in the news. She glanced briefly over the different headlines and when she was done she got up to make some coffee. She would have to go over to The Inn to grab some breakfast since she had yet to go pick up some groceries. Picking up her keys and purse she started to head out but decided to grab her tablet too and work on some of her designs while she ate.

Twenty minutes later she was seated at a small table by the window at The Inn's restaurant, enjoying her second cup of coffee that morning and a plate full of fresh fruit and croissants. As she ate she browsed through some websites for materials she would need for the new décor in The Inn. She was so intent on deciding which light fixtures she would like to use for the front foyer that she did not notice someone stopping beside her table. It wasn't until she heard someone clearing their throat that she looked up to see Jake standing there.

"Oh, hi Jake, I didn't see you there," Alexis said surprised.

"It's okay. I saw you sitting here and thought I would stop by to say hi," Jake replied.

"That was nice of you, would you like to sit?"

"Sure, I can stay for a few minutes," he said siting down. "I see you got one of the houses favourites for breakfast."

"Yes, and it's delicious. Would you like some?" she asked pushing the plate towards him.

"No thanks. I had a big breakfast with Becky this morning so I'm good until lunch time, but I will get a coffee. I'll just go get one, I'll be right back."

Alexis watched him go to the kitchen and admired the way his body moved and how well his jeans fit, especially in the lower area. Shaking her head she tried to think of something else before her thoughts got her in trouble. She picked up a strawberry and looked out the window at the small lake. It was a beautiful morning, the sun was shining, and the lake was calm. It wasn't a big lake, but she could see that there were a few canoes along the shore for those that wanted to just go out for a little bit of fun. You would never guess that this little hidden gem was at the edge of the town. Her grandparents had been lucky in being able to acquire this place all those years.

Thinking of her grandparents, she realized that the end of this summer would mark their fiftieth anniversary. She would have to think of something special to do for them and what to get them. Their anniversary wasn't until September third which this year landed in the Labour Day weekend. Yes, she would definitely have to think of something special. Maybe she could get the renovations done by then and have a party here at The Inn for them. It sounded like a great idea and she smiled at the prospect of doing this for them.

"A penny for the beautiful woman's thoughts?" Jake asked sitting down across form her.

Alexis blushed at this and that made Jake smile. "I was just thinking of my grandparents and the fact that it's their fiftieth anniversary coming up in a couple of months," she said, composing herself.

"Wow, I didn't realize that was this year. It's nice to see that love can last for some people, and I don't know of a more deserving couple than those two. I would love to have what they have."

"I think everyone does, but for some it's not meant to be."

Jake could hear the bitterness in her voice as she stated the last part. "I take it someone broke your heart?" he asked

"You could say that. But looking back at it now, I wonder if I really did love Frank. I think I might have been in love with the life he led and they people he knew and the places we went."

"Do you mind if I ask what happened?"

Alexis didn't answer right away. She thought about how opening up to him yesterday had helped her and maybe having someone to talk to about Frank would help her as well. There was also the fact that for some reason, she felt comfortable with Jake and opened up to him ways that she had never been able to do with another man before. Decision made, she took a deep breath then proceeded to tell Jake her story.

Jake listened as Alexis told him her story of how she had met Frank, a successful business owner and how she had fallen for his charms. Frank had treated her like a princess and had given her everything, taken her to exotic places for vacation and introduced her to his friends, which included some celebrities. Later they had gone into business together when he offered to finance an Interior Design Company for her. Although she only had a few employees, but she had made a name for herself, and even landed a few jobs for some high-profile people. She admitted to him that she might have only got those clients because of Frank. Eventually they had got engaged and Alexis had felt like her life was perfect. She had been mistaken. Frank had changed after that and he had become more distant. They went out less and didn't travel as much as they once had. His attitude towards her had changed and he became confrontational and more distant. She found out that he was having an affair with a few other women and she had ended it with him. But it didn't end there. She also found out that he had been embezzling money through her company and when the authorities finally caught up with him she lost her business and all its assets. By the time it was done she had lost everything, and Frank had ended up in jail. She had sold her house to pay off the debts and made the decision to move Silver Springs when her grandparents had offered her a job renovating The Inn.

Jake let out a low whistle as Alexis finished her story. He admired her even more now that he knew what she had gone through over the last few years on top of her revelations from yesterday. He didn't know many people that would have been able to endure all that she had gone through and still be able to function. This was definitely one strong woman sitting across the table from him.

"I feel like you should be charging me an hourly rate with everything I've been unloading on you in the last twenty-four hours," Alexis said with a laugh.

"Don't worry, I don't mind listening and I'm sure I can come up with something to make up for my time," he joked.

Alexis laughed too and then she noticed that there was something beside him wrapped in a brown paper bag. What's that?" she asked curiously nodding toward the bag.

"Oh this, I almost forgot! Samantha dropped this off to me this morning to give to you. She meant to give it to last night, but she forgot to."

"For me, really? I wonder what it could be?"

Jake slid it across the table to her. "Why don't you open it and find out."

Alexis picked up the bag and looked in it curiously. She pulled out a book and turned it over looking at the cover. "I can't believe it!" she said in surprise.

"What is it?" Jake asked

"This is the book that I was going to buy yesterday at her store, but I put it down on top of a shelf when I left. I wonder how she knew about this?"

"My guess would be Becky. Not much gets by her and she did see what happened yesterday, so my guess is that she saw you put that book down and told Samantha."

"I honestly don't know what to say. This is a kindness that I just don't know how to react to. I have never experienced this before," Alexis said with a glimmer of tears coming to her eyes.

"I think a simple thank you would suffice. Samantha has a big heart and she likes you. Plus as I'm sure you are learning, here in Silver Springs we take care of each other, it's something you will have to get used to."

Alexis looked up at Jake in and wonder, and he leaned across the table to wipe her tears away with his napkin. He hated to see her cry but at least this time it was tears of joy for her. She smiled at him hesitantly and their eyes locked for a moment before he sat back in his chair.

To the casual observer, they would look like a couple in love sharing a private moment and it was that moment that Susan observed from the main entry to the restaurant. She smiled to herself and walked away before the two of them noticed her there. She walked back to her office where Becky was waiting for her and knew that her instincts that Alexis and Jake would make a good match was correct. Maybe there was hope for them both to still find love in each other, since they both had been through so much and deserved to be happy. She wanted to see Alexis happy again and her granddaughter was quickly coming out of her depression since arriving here, and it had only been three days. Yes, making up the excuse that The Inn needed to be renovated and asking Alexis to come do it had been the perfect idea she thought to herself. She hoped to have Alexis settled with Jake by the end of the summer when her and Marty made their surprise plans public to everyone.

After Alexis and Jake had finished their coffees they went their separate ways, Jake to go do the paperwork he had not finished yesterday and Alexis to go order some materials she needed. They had agreed to meet up at five o'clock when Jake was done work, so he could show her around town and take her to the local grocery store, so she could get some much-needed food for her cabin.

Alexis was happy with the how her morning had gone, and she was sure she had been right in opening up once more to Jake, it had felt right. He was a man that she knew she could count on and would always be a good friend. She spent the next couple of hours online ordering fabrics, light fixtures, flooring and a few other things she needed for the makeover of the inside of The Inn. Jake had agreed to contact a local contractor for her to come over tomorrow and give her some quotes on the new renovations she had in mind.

Everything was falling into place for her renovations and when she was finished she took her new book, a blanket from the sofa and a bottle of water and went to go sit by the pond and read for a few hours. At the edge of the pond she laid her blanket out on the grass and sat down with her book. Time slipped by on her as she became engrossed in her book and a couple hours passed before she stopped to take a break. She lay back on her blanket and watched the few clouds floating by before a large shadow blocked the sunlight. She turned her head to the side and was rewarded with a lick to the face by Max.

"Ugh, Max, that's disgusting," Alexis sputtered as she tried to sit up.

Max wagged his tail madly and nudged her with his muzzle wanting attention. He refused to move so Alexis gave in and scratched his ear because she knew he liked that. That made Max happy and he sat down leaning into her. Alexis laughed at him and she wondered where he had come from. She had not seen him when she had come out a couple hours ago, so someone must be home. She looked towards the cabin but didn't see anyone so maybe she was wrong. Soon Max was lying down beside her and wanted his belly scratched, so she complied. As she was rubbing his stomach she heard Becky calling his name.

"Max, where did you go?" Becky called again.

Max ignored the girls call, being too content to stay where he was. "Max, Becky wants you," Alexis said, giving the dog a little shove but he refused to move. "Becky, he's over her," she called out when Max refused to return to Becky.

"There you are Max," Becky said running into the clearing from the path that led to The Inn. "I was wondering why you didn't come back when I called you, but I can see why now. Hi Miss Alexis."

"Hi Becky. What are you up to this afternoon?"

"Not much now. Max and I were with Grandma Susan most of the day and now we wanted to come back and play here for a while. Grandpa Marty will be here soon, he couldn't keep up with us."

"No, I'm sure he couldn't. What are you going to play?"

"Oh, I'm not sure. A lot of the time Grandpa Marty and I will walk the paths around here and he'll teach me about the different plants, or we throw the baseball, or he sits and reads while I draw things in my sketch pad."

"That sounds nice. I used to do a lot of those things with him as well when I was you're age. Do you ever go swimming in the lake behind The Inn?"

"Gosh no, it's too cold for me!"

"That's half the fun though, I used to love going in and today would be a perfect day for that, its sunny and warm."

"But that lake is mountain water, I'll freeze in there."

"I found the trick was that if you kept moving then you stayed warm, it was only if you stayed still that it got cold."

"Really?"

"Yes really. If you want I can take you some time, you can swim right?"

"Oh yes I can. I've taken lessons every year since I was three in the summers since we can't swim in the winter because the pool is an outdoor one. Although they are talking about building a new Rec Center that would have an indoor pool. You should ask Brian about that, since he's on the community council now and knows more about it."

"That would be wonderful if they did do that. I always thought that Silver Springs needed an indoor pool."

"Alexis…"

"Yes Becky?"

"Will you take me to the lake now? Now that you've talked about it I'd like to go try it, that is if you will take me," Becky asked hesitantly with a hopeful look on her face.

Alexis looked up at the little girl that was staring at her shoes as she waited for an answer. She was thrilled that the girl wanted to do something with her and the look on her face made it hard to say no. "I don't see why we can't. We still have lots of time before I have to meet up with your dad."

"Oh wow Miss Alexis, you're the best!" Becky cried out as she knelt down and threw her arms around her.

"And why is my beautiful granddaughter the best?" Marty asked coming up to them.

"She's going to take me swimming in the lake right now. I have to go get my bathing suit on, I'll be right back!" Becky gushed as she got up and raced towards the cabin before she was even done her sentence.

"She's really taken a shine to you Lexi," Marty said using his nickname for her. "She swore she would never go in that lake because it was too cold for her."

"Yes, well I'm fond of her too. She's a good kid," Alexis said, getting up and collecting her things.

"That she is. She's had a lonely childhood and she's never had a mother at her side, and I think she sees what she never had in you."

"Really, you think so Gramps?"

"Yes I do. Listen Lexi, I'm going to be honest with you since your Grandma isn't her to tell me to mind my own business. Your Grandma has it in her head that you and Jake would make a good pair and is determined to see the two of you together. The only reason I'm telling you this is because I don't want to see that little girl get hurt.

Jake's a big boy and take care of himself, but Becky is sweet and innocent. Like I said, I just don't want to see her get hurt."

"I understand Gramps, and I figured it out yesterday what Grandma is up to. I just haven't decided what to think of it yet. I mean I like Jake, but as a friend. Right now I don't see myself being anything more than a friend to him, although who knows what the future might bring. I've learned in the last few days that my outlook on life is changing and who knows what tomorrow will bring. But I can tell you this, I like Becky and I will never do anything to hurt her, or Jake."

"That's my girl. I knew you were a smart one and I thought you might have figured it out yesterday, but I wasn't sure so that's why I brought it up. Oh and you might want to know that Becky figured out what your Grandma was up to and she's in on it now too. I think Jake is the only one who doesn't know," Marty said laughing.

"Why am I not surprised," Alexis said laughing as well. "I love you Gramps and I'm glad to be back here," she added.

"Me too Lexi, me too," he said giving her a hug.

Alexis walked back to her cabin to get changed after she told her grandpa that she would meet them over by the lake in ten minutes. She put her things down in the cabin and looked around trying to figure out if she had brought a swim suit with her or if it was in with the rest of her belongings that would arrive in a few days. She searched through her clothes and not finding one she picked out a pair of black active wear shorts and top to wear instead. She grabbed a large fluffy towel from her bathroom, her sunglasses and sandals, then headed out again to meet Becky and her grandpa over at the lake.

Alexis was looking forward to a swim in the lake and was happy that Becky had suggested it. It had been a long time since she had done this, and she was determined to show the girl that cold water could be fun!

Chapter Nine

Jake was sitting at his desk writing out some checks when he heard a high pitch scream come from outside that made the hairs on the back of his neck standup. He knew that scream, it was Becky's and he shot of his chair to look out the window behind him. He couldn't see much through the large tree that was in front of him, but he was sure that the sound had come from the vicinity of the lake. Scared that she might have fallen in, he grabbed his cellphone and raced out of his office to the nearest exit to the back of the property.

Rushing out the door he heard Becky scream again but this time it was followed by laughter. What the hell, he thought to himself as he rounded the building and started down the manicured lawn towards the lake. He stopped abruptly about twenty feet from the lakes edge and stared in disbelief at the scene in front of him.

Becky was in the lake and was splashing Alexis, who was in turn splashing her back while Max swam between them They were chasing each other around and Marty was sitting in a lounge chair by the side of the lake watching and smiling.

"What was all that screaming?" Susan asked rushing up to Jakes side then stopping as she looked towards the lake as well. "Is that Becky and Alexis in the lake?"

"It would appear so," Jake replied still watching them.

"I almost had a heart attack when I heard Becky scream the first time. I thought maybe she had fallen in the lake."

"That was my thought too Susan."

"But I thought she hated the lake because it was too cold to swim in?"

"So did I, but apparently she's changed her mind, and I have a feeling I know why," Jake said letting his gaze stop on Alexis.

Jake watched Alexis and thought that she was absolutely beautiful at that moment and his heart skipped a beat. Her hair was wet and tousled, and she was smiling radiantly. Whatever she was wearing was clinging to her slim body and it made Jakes body stir in desire. In that moment as he watched her play with his daughter, he knew that he wanted to try to be more than just friends with her. Not because of the way she looked but because of the open kindness and friendship that she continued to show his daughter. No one had ever truly done that to this extent, and for that he knew that she was the one he had been waiting for all these years.

"I'm sure if you ask her out to dinner she'd say yes," Susan told to him as she watched him watch her granddaughter.

"What do you mean?" Jake asked, turning to look at Susan.

"I can see the way you've been looking at her. I can tell your attracted to Alexis and I'm saying that if you asked her out she would probably say yes because I've seen the way she looks at you to."

"I'm not sure, she's made it clear she's only looking for a friendship right now."

"Oh pish posh, I'm sure once she spends more time with you that she'll change her mind. Aren't you supposed to be taking her shopping later?"

"Umm, yes I am, I didn't realize you knew that."

"There's not much around here that I don't know about," Susan laughed as she saw the surprised look on his face. "When you're out, why don't you casually suggest stopping to eat somewhere. Marty and I will watch Becky at our place and make her dinner as well."

Jake looked hard at Susan. He was beginning to think that he was being set up by the old women if he wasn't mistaken. Between yesterday at lunch and now he was thinking he might be right. He didn't say anything but turned to watch Alexis and Becky again who were idly swimming around the small lake. It was Becky who spotted him first.

"Daddy! Come down and see me swim! Miss Alexis told me how to stay warm when we're in here and its great!" Becky called out as she swam towards the shore.

"I'm coming Sweat-Pea!" Jake called back.

"Think about what I said," Susan reminded him then turned and headed over to where Marty was sitting.

"Daddy, the lake is great once you get used to it!" Becky said as she waded out of the water.

"It looks like you were having a great time! I never would have believed it was you in there until you called out, I'm proud of you," Jake said giving his wet daughter a hug.

"Oh Daddy, you should come in, it's so much fun and Miss Alexis is so much fun to swim with. Although I'll warn you it's cold when you first get in. I screamed when I jumped in."

"So that's why I heard you screaming all the way from the office. It sounded like you were in trouble and you scared me to death."

"I'm sorry Daddy, you aren't mad at me are you?"

"Of course not Sweat-Pea, I'm glad that you're having fun. But you're shivering, you should go get your towel."

"No way Daddy, I'm going back in, you should come too," she called out as she ran back into the water where Alexis was waiting for her.

"Another time, I don't have a swim suit with me."

"Okay, how about tomorrow afternoon?"

"Sounds good to me!"

Becky continued to play with Alexis and Jake went over to where Marty and Susan were sitting. He sat down in a chair and watched his daughter. She was having the time of her life and he loved how much she had opened up in the past few days, which was all due to Alexis. Normally she would have been playing quietly or drawing something. She didn't have a lot of friends and tended to be an introvert the majority of the time. It warmed his heart to see her this way and he was thinking that maybe he should listen to what Susan had suggested. He would see how things went with Alexis when they went out later before he asked her anything.

The two out in the lake swam and played for another fifteen minutes before they both came out shivering, saying that they had had enough. Susan immediately grabbed the towels and handed one to Jake, nodding toward Alexis, and took the other one to wrap Becky in. Taking the hint, he took the towel and got up to go over to where Alexis was.

"Here you go," he said quietly as he wrapped the towel around her and stepped back.

"Why thank you Jake, that was nice of you to bring me the towel, I'm freezing now that I'm out of the water," Alexis said giving her arms and body a vigorous rub with the towel.

"You're welcome, it looked like you were having fun."

"Oh yes, we were. Becky is so much fun to be with and I'm glad she suggested we go swimming after I told her about how I used to go in all the time when I was her age."

"Really? Well I'm happy that you were the one to take her, she really likes you."

Alexis smiled at him while she continued to dry her hair with her towel. Up close Jake noticed just how toned Alexis's body was and thought that she must work out. He itched to reach out a hand and touch her exposed skin but restrained himself from doing that. He also wanted to kiss her and taste those full lips of hers. She must have seen the look on his face because she stopped drying herself off and looked at him.

"Is something wrong Jake?" She asked.

"Umm, what? No, I'm good," he said.

"Are you sure? You have this look on your face like you want to say or do something."

"I bet he wants to kiss you!" Becky chimed in as she walked up to them.

"Becky!" both Alexis and Jake said at the same time.

"What, wouldn't you like to kiss her Daddy, she is very pretty," Becky went on innocently.

Jake glanced at Alexis embarrassed and he could hear both Marty and Susan chuckling behind him and he groaned. Alexis looked both shocked and embarrassed just like him.

"Becky shouldn't you go get changed before you get cold?" Jake said giving her a look.

"I guess Daddy, but I really think you should kiss her," she added before she sprinted off towards their cabin with Marty following behind her at a slower pace.

"I'm sorry Alexis, Becky tends to be a little outspoken at times," Jake said in the way of an apology to her for his daughter's rash behaviour.

"It's okay Jake, she just caught me by surprise, and you too by the looks of it," Alexis said as she wrapped the towel around herself and put her sandals back on.

"So you're not upset with her then?"

"No, why would I be? She's just being herself and wishing that her daddy will kiss the pretty lady that took her swimming," Alexis responded laughing. "Besides, I would be so lucky to be kissed by Silver Springs most eligible bachelor and be envied by all the woman in town!"

Jake did not know what to say that and stared at her with his mouth hanging open.

"Score one for my granddaughter," Susan said giving him a knowing look. That made him shut his mouth. "Becky wants to stay with us tonight, so we told her she could, and we'll bring her home in the morning," Susan added as she gave him a last look then left them to go follow her husband and Becky.

"What was that all about?" Alexis asked.

"You don't want to know," Jake replied and let out a little sigh.

"Actually I have a feeling I might know."

"What do you mean?"

"I think my Grandma and Becky have been scheming on how to get the two of us together."

Jake looked at her, surprised that she had voiced what he had been suspecting. "That's what I was thinking too."

"So what do you want to do about it?" Alexis asked going to sit in one of the chairs that her grandparents had just been sitting in.

"I don't know," he said running his fingers through his hair and going to sit down beside her.

"What if we played along with it?" Alexis said, surprising him.

"You're not serious are you?"

"Yes. If my Grandma wants to meddle in our lives why not have some fun with it."

"Well, it could be fun," he said as he thought about how he had wanted to kiss her earlier. Plus maybe this would be the opportunity he was looking for to see if he could win her over to being more than just friends. A slow smile spread across his face as the idea appealed to him even more. "Let's do it. But how do you propose that we go about doing this?"

"I'm not sure yet, I mean we're friends and we're going to have to make it look like there's more to it, plus we have to still maintain a professional working relationship. So it has to be a balance of all of that. But there is just one flaw in all of this."

"And what would that be?"

"Becky."

"Oh. I forgot about that for a moment. Maybe we shouldn't do this because I don't want to get her hopes up and potentially hurt her. That wouldn't be fair to her."

"Agreed. It's too bad it could have been fun to teach my Grandma a lesson. Maybe we can come up with something else."

"Yes, maybe," Jake replied, silently wishing they could have gone through with it. Now he would have to think of a different way to win her over since she had once again made it clear that they were friends and had to maintain a professional working relationship. Where his hopes had been high a minute ago, they were now low again. But when it came to Becky, her well being came before anything else.

"Well I guess I should go get changed if you're going to show me around town and then take me to the store," Alexis said getting up.

"Yeah, and I have to go finish what I was doing before I came running out here."

"Okay, I'll meet you at your place in half an hour then?"

"Sounds good, see you then."

They shared a look and then Alexis turned to walk back to her cabin. Jake watched her go wishing that he could have more with this woman. It had only been three days, but he was sure that she had already stolen his heart. Who would have thought that the woman who had showed up a few days ago could be the same one that had just walked away from him? He turned to walk back to his office and tried to think of a way to turn the tide in his favour.

Once in his office he sat down at his desk and swiveled his chair, so he could look out the window. His mind was not on work and he doubted he would get anything else done today, he would just have to come in early tomorrow to play catch up. He wracked his brain trying to figure out how he could make Alexis see that they could be more than friends. He thought back on the suggestions he had gotten from both Brian and Susan over the last twenty-four hours and that's when the glimmer of an idea started to form. He let the idea grow until he had it and a smile formed on his face. He turned back to the desk and picked up the phone, punching in the numbers to Sam's. He was going to need his friends help with his plan.

Alexis decided to have a quick shower when she got back to the cabin because she needed to cool off again. That brief interlude with Jake and talk of pretending to be a couple had brought images to her mind that had flustered her. What is wrong with you? Alexis thought to herself.

"You don't need to be thinking of him that way right now. A relationship, even pretend, is the last thing you need right now after Frank," the practical part of her mind screamed.

"But he's not Frank," the other part of her mind shot back.

"Yes, but you have to work with him, so keep it professional."

"But he's proven he's a good man and I feel at ease with him, something I've never felt with another man before."

"So, he's still a man, and he will hurt you just like the others."

'No he, won't."

"Would you two shut up!" Alexis said tuning off the shower and getting out to dry off.

Alexis tried not to think about it any more as he applied some makeup and quickly dried her hair. She chose a summer dress to wear and a pair of matching sandals. Taking one last look in the mirror, she decided that she was ready and grabbed her purse and sunglasses and headed off to Jake's cabin.

Jake saw Alexis coming across the lawn and went outside to meet her on the deck. She looked beautiful in her dress and her hair hanging loosely down her back. She would not be considered tall as she was only about five foot six inches he guessed but he thought she was the perfect height for him. As she walked up the stairs towards him, he smiled at her and she smiled back which made everything seem brighter to him.

"Hello Alexis," he said as she stopped in front of him.

"Hi Jake," she answered taking in his fresh attire and damp hair. "Are you ready to go?"

"Sure, we can go around to the back where my car is parked.

Alexis followed him and is car turned out to be a beautiful black Jeep with the hard cover taken off at the moment.

"This is yours?" she asked as she admired it.

"Yes."

"I like it."

"Thank you, I find it's great for when I want to go off roading to go camping or hiking."

"Do you do that a lot?" Alexis asked as she climbed in after Jake thoughtfully opened the door for her.

"Yes, or at least I try to. Being the Manager at The Inn and being a fulltime parent takes up a lot of my time, so I don't get out as much as I would like. But Becky and I go whenever we can. We're actually going camping up at Silver Lake next weekend. It should be fun."

"That does sound like fun, I'm sure you two will have a great time."

"Yes. So where do you want to go first?" Jake asked getting into the Jeep and starting it.

"I'm not sure. What do you suggest?"

"I was thinking that we could walk through the town first. I'm sure a few things have changed since you were last here. I do need to pick up a book for Becky that came in for her at Sam's if you don't mind?"

"Not at all, that will actually give me a chance to thank Samantha for the book."

"Great, after that we can decide where you want to go from there." Jake was pleased that she had wanted to go to Sam's as that fell into his plans that he had made earlier in his office. He put he Jeep into drive and he drove down the long driveway that brought them out to a side road that would take them to town.

Chapter Ten

Alexis got out of the Jeep when they arrived in town and she looked towards the river admiring the beauty of it and the surrounding park.

"Gramps used to bring me down here all the time when I was a girl and we would go fishing over there," Alexis said pointing to where the bend in the river was.

"That's a good fishing spot, I used to fish there too as a kid and now I fish there with Becky," Jake said, coming around to Jeep to stand beside her. "Did you keep the fish or was it strictly catch and release?"

"Catch and release, I didn't want to clean them."

"That's the same as Becky, she never lets me keep any of the fish we catch."

"Smart girl."

They stood there and watched the river flow by them for a minute before setting off to walk down the street. Jake pointed out the new businesses and shops as well as the old ones and Alexis would point out the odd place that she remembered. They walked to the end of the street then turned and headed into the park. The flower beds were a riot of different colours and couples were lounging on blankets spread out on the grass while families were playing and having a great time.

Alexis had loved this park as a child and even though it wasn't that big she had thought then that it was and that it was enchanted. She smiled at the memory and Jake noticed the happy look on her face.

"Remembering something?" he asked

"Yes, just some memories from when I was a child," she responded and told him about what she had been thinking.

Jake led her to a nearby bench and sat down with her as she told stories about playing here with her grandparents and how her grandma would pretend to be her fairy godmother. Her grandpa would hide in the bushes and jump out pretending to be a troll and scare her. She had loved those times and a small part of her wished she could go back to those care free days. They sat there quietly in quiet contemplation for a few minutes before Alexis noticed the bench they were sitting on.

"This is a beautiful bench and it looks new," she commented as she leaned forward to admire the intricate workmanship that had been put into it.

"Yes, it's not that old," Jake said, and Alexis noted a hint of sadness in his voice.

"What is it Jake?"

"This bench means a lot to the people of Silver Springs," he said taking her hand and helping her up. He then turned and pointed to the two plaques on the bench. "This bench was put here in remembrance of two of Silver Springs best paramedics that lost their lives earlier this year."

"Oh Jake, what happened?"

Jake went on to tell her about Keith and Jamie and the sad story of how they had passed away. Alexis listened, and she instinctively squeezed his hand that she was still holding. She could tell that the town had been heartbroken at the loss of these two men, and that Jake felt that pain too. She took a closer look at the plaques and the one name seemed to stand out, but it took her a minute to figure out why. She gasped when she made the connection.

"Keith has the same last name as Brian. He's the brother that he lost earlier this year isn't it?" she asked.

"Yes it is, and it almost broke him. If it hadn't been for Samantha I don't know if he could have survived the loss of his brother. They were very close, and Keith was also Samantha's best friend. Inadvertently, Keith's passing is what brought Brain and Samantha back together."

"Oh that's so heart breaking, for both of them. Were you close to either of these men?"

"No, not really. I mean, I knew both of them, but Keith was older than me and Jamie had only lived here a few years."

"Oh."

"Come on, lets go walk some more and then head over to Sam's," Jake said giving her hand a little tug.

Alexis followed after taking one last look at the bench. They exited the park and walked slowly down the street then turned onto the main road that all the popular shops and businesses were on. People that passed them smiled and the odd one said hello, and in general the people of Silver Springs were very friendly Alexis thought. How could she have thought this was a horrible place all these years. She had been blinded by one misdeed and blamed the whole town, which wasn't right.

Alexis noticed however that a few people gave them bigger smiles than others did, and she couldn't figure out why until some stranger in a truck drove by and yelled, "It's about damn time Jake!" and honked his horn. This earned them a few more smiles.

"What was that all about?" Alexis asked.

"I'm not sure," Jake said looking after the truck.

"Well I see Jake has finally come to his senses," a male voice said from behind them.

They turned around to find Brian standing in a doorway with a big smile on his face.

"What do you mean, come to his senses?" Alexis asked when she saw who it was.

"Silver Springs most eligible bachelor has finally come out of hibernation and has shown an interest in a woman, and a beautiful one at that," Brain said looking downwards.

They both followed his gaze and saw that they were still holding hands. They had been walking through town like this and had not even realized it. Looking up they gazed into each other's eyes and smiled. It felt right and neither of them made a move to let go.

"Well now, are you two just going to stare at each other all day and block the door to my office or are you going to move?" Brain asked with a laugh. Alexis and Jake laughed along with him and moved so Brain get all the way out of his door to stand beside them. "What brings you two to town?"

"Jake was showing me the town and then we were going to stop by Sam's then go shopping," Alexis answered. "We just came from the park and I saw the bench. It's a beautiful way to remember your brother by."

"Thank you, I think so too," Brain said with a look of both sadness and contentment on his handsome face. "Well, I was on my way to Sam's too, so I'll walk with you there."

The three of them headed off down the street to walk the short distance to Samantha's store. It was just as busy as it has been the last time Alexis had been there and it took them a minute to get in and make their way to the back of the store where they waited for Samantha to finish up with her customers. Once she was free she joined the others.

"I want to thank you for your gift of the book Samantha, it was a very generous thing to do," Alexis said after getting an impromptu hug from Samantha, something that she was not used to, but decided that she liked.

"You're welcome. It's the least I could do after what happened to you in my store. Come, I'll show you around while the guys talk," Samantha said, taking her hand and leading her away from the men.

Jake watched them disappear into the back of the store before turning to Brian. "Well, that went well but not the way I had planned it," he said.

"Nothing ever goes the way you plan it Jake, I've learned that over this last year. Besides, it doesn't look like you need our help now, it seems like things are falling into place for you on their own," Brian said with a chuckle.

"Yes, it does seem that way, but let's see how it goes, I may need your help still. Let's go get a coffee while we wait for them to come back. I have a feeling they will be awhile if I know your wife!"

Brian laughed, and they went to stand in line for their coffees. Jake liked Brian and even though they had only recently become good friends, he counted him as one of his best friends now. Brian was older than him, but they had much in common and it was one of the reasons they had become friends. He had known Samantha all his life and had been acquaintances, but now he counted her as one of his closest friends as well. Friends were something he did not have a lot of and he liked it that way, as he was a very private person.

When the two had finally gotten their coffees there was no where to sit so they decided to go outside to wait for the women. They found one table outside that had only just been vacated and sat down before anyone else could take it. There they talked about nothing of importance and waited for Alexis and Samantha.

"So spill it," Samantha said as soon as she had shown Alexis her private office up stairs. "How did you do it?"

"Excuse me?" Alexis asked confused. "How did I do what?"

"Jake? You have Jake head over heals for you, I can see it in his eyes and the way he looks at you."

"Well I don't know about that, I mean I know he likes me, but I wouldn't say head over heals."

"Are you blind girl? That man is falling in love with you! I've known Jake my whole life and I have never seen him this way before, not even with Becky's mom. He has been Silver Springs most elusive bachelor for the last seven years and he always made it clear that he had no intentions of dating anyone until the right woman came along for him and Becky. Apparently you're it."

"You can't be serious? I mean, we've only known each other for three days now, and I have to admit we didn't hit it off right away. But he is a nice guy and I like him, but I'm not interested in anything serious right now."

"Girl you are blind, because I not only see how he feels but I can see it in you too. I saw the way he was holding your hand and the way you smile at him. You're falling for him, even if you won't admit it to yourself."

"But we barely know each other…"

"It doesn't matter. When two people are destined for each other it doesn't matter what you do or think, you can't change Destiny's mind, and I think she has her eye set on the two of you being together. Why else do you think Jake has broken his seven-year streak of not being interested in anyone? Why have you been spending most of your time with him? Why were you so comfortable opening up to him but no one else about what happened all those years ago? You two are meant for each other and I think you will see that soon too."

Alexis sat down on the sofa as she digested what Samantha had just said. It was true, all of it, but was she ready to accept that? Could things really happen that fast? She had heard about that happening to others, but she had never really truly believed in Destiny or Fate. But now here she was in that position and it scared her. She was supposed to be here to work with Jake, not fall for him. She had already had one relationship fail with someone she had worked with, so hadn't she learned her lesson? But he's different she thought, for the second time that day.

"I can see that you're having a hard time digesting what I just told you, and don't worry, it's okay to be scared. If you weren't I would wonder what was wrong with you. Nothing says you have to act right away, just take some time to think about it and enjoy your time with him."

"Thanks Samantha, I will," Alexis said closing her eyes.

Samantha left Alexis to her thoughts and sat down at her desk to wait. She picked up her favourite book that was sitting on her desk and skimmed through it as she waited.

Twenty minutes later the guys got up from their table when they saw Samantha and Alexis come outside. Jake immediately noticed a slight change in Alexis and wondered what the two women had been talking about, but if he had to venture a guess he'd bet it was about him. Just as he and Brian had eventually brought their conversation back to her.

He went over to her and she smiled shyly at him and his heart warmed at the sight. He then gently took her hand and she did not pull back, which was a good sign.

"So what were you two girls up too? It felt like we were waiting forever," Brian teased.

"Well you know us women, we like to keep you men waiting," Samantha shot back.

"I'd wait forever for you, and you know that."

Samantha laughed and hugged her husband then gave him a quick kiss. "So did you ask Jake?"

"Ask me what?" Jake asked innocently.

"We're going for dinner up at the Silver Mountain Ski Resort, and we were wondering if you would like to join us, and Alexis too?" Samantha asked.

"I'm not sure, it depends on what Alexis would like to do?" Jake answered, as they all looked to Alexis.

"Actually I was hoping to go get my groceries after this and then I thought if Jake was up for it I would like to make him dinner to say thank you for all his help and kindness he's shown me over the past few days," Alexis said quietly.

"Well of course Jake would like that, wouldn't you Jake?" Samantha said with a mischievous grin.

"Don't you think you should give him a chance to answer for himself dear?" Brain admonished his wife.

"I would love that Alexis," Jake answered her, ignoring his two friends. "I would rather spend an evening with you than these two old wind bags any day," he added.

"Hey, we're not that old," Brian shot back.

"Old enough my friend. Are you ready to go now Alexis?" Jake asked.

"Yes," Alexis answered both amused at the teasing between friends and a little embarrassed about being the center of everyone's attention.

"Great! Samantha, I see you have Becky's book there, so I'll take it and give it to her tomorrow," Jake said taking the book from her.

"Tomorrow?" Samantha asked

"Yes, she's staying with Susan and Marty tonight, so I won't see her until sometime tomorrow morning," Jake replied.

"I see. Then what are you two still doing here?" Samantha asked giving them both a little shove to get them moving. "Go enjoy a kid free night and some peace and quiet."

"See you guys around," Brian called out as they walked away.

Jake gave him a look over his should and Brian winked at him and Samantha was still grinning. It turned out he didn't need their help after all.

An hour later found Jake unloading Alexis groceries while she played with Max who had come to greet them when they got home. He wasn't sure how he had been stuck with this job, but he didn't mind if it meant that he would get to spend more time alone with Alexis. He put all the groceries on her table, not knowing where she wanted to put everything then was about to head back out when she came in.

"He's so full of energy, I can't keep up with him. I think given the chance he would never stop playing," Alexis said out of breath.

"Yes, I imagine he would and that's one of the reasons why he's so good for Becky," Jake answered. "Where is he now?"

"I'm not sure? He took off down the path towards The Inn."

"He probably went back to find Becky. He'll go with her to Marty and Susan's for the night. I left all the groceries out, do you want some help putting them away?"

"No, I think I should be good. Once I'm done I'll start dinner, I hope you're hungry."

"I'm starved, I haven't eaten since this morning."

"Then I guess I better start here so you don't starve to death on my watch," she teased. "Do you have a good bottle of white wine to go with dinner? I never thought to stop at the liquor store on the way home."

"I'm sure I do, I'll go check to see what I have, and I'll be back in a few minutes."

"Sounds good."

Alexis quickly put all the groceries away then she started preparing dinner. She had opted to make a seafood linguini and had a loaf of French bread that she was going to turn into garlic bread. By the time Jake came back dinner was coming along nicely, and she stopped to take the glass of wine that Jake had just poured for her. They clinked glasses and sipped the delicious wine.

"Smells good in here. I don't think I've ever had homemade seafood pasta before," Jake said as he leaned against the counter.

"Then you're in for a treat, it's one of my favourite dishes to make," she replied as she stirred the pot of boiling pasta.

"If it tastes as good as it looks then you can cook for me any day."

Alexis laughed, and Jake joined in too. He loved the sound of her laugh and also the way her whole face lite up when she smiled. Right now he wanted nothing more than to take her into his arms and kiss her. But he had a feeling now was not the time to act on such a feeling. He would wait until later, if he felt that she was ready, as he didn't want to scare her away. They would have dinner and see where the night went from there.

Dinner was perfect. Alexis had arranged for them to eat at her small table that still had Becky's flowers on it and she had also added some candles she had purchased at the store. They ate the seafood linguini, to which Jake declared was the best he had ever tasted and drank more of the wine he had brought.

When dinner was over they quickly cleared the dishes and loaded then into the small dishwasher and left the pots for later. They took what was left of the wine and sat down on the sofa and put their feet up on the coffee table. The curtains were still open, and they looked out to into the fading night and watched the ducks on the pond.

"Thank you for everything today Jake, I really enjoyed myself and being with you," Alexis said breaking the silence.

"And I enjoyed being with you too," he answered looking at her.

"I feel so comfortable with you. We've only known each other for a few days but it feels like it's been a lot longer than that."

"I know what you mean, I feel the same way."

"Do you know what Samantha said to me today?"

"No, but I'm guessing it had something to do with Destiny?"

"How did you know that?" Alexis asked surprised.

"For as long as I've known Samantha, she's always believed in Destiny and Fate. She believes it what brought her and Brian back together after all those years they spent apart. I'm guessing that she believes we're destined to be together as well?"

"Exactly right. I don't know if I believe in Destiny like she does but some of the things she said today made sense and to be honest, I don't know what to think quite yet."

Jake turned sideways to look at Alexis and saw the confusion of what was happening between them on her face. He searched her eyes that looked hopefully to him for answers, before he leaned in and gently kissed her on the lips.

Chapter Eleven

Her lips were soft and at first she didn't respond, but after a moment of hesitation she kissed him back. Jake groaned as she responded to him and he deepened the kiss. His fingers tangled into her hair at the back of her head and he pulled her in closer. She whimpered slightly, and he pulled back, searching her face to make sure she was okay. She looked to him with passion filled eyes and he couldn't stop himself from kissing her again.

Alexis wrapped her arms around him and savoured the kiss. She felt like she was on fire and her body was reacting to him in so many different ways. It had been a long time since she had felt desire for anyone, but what she was feeling now didn't even compare to any of her experiences before. She wanted more. She wanted to feel his skin against hers and started pulling his shirt out of the waistband of his pants. Soon she had it untucked, and to pull it over his head she had to break contact with him but only for a quick moment. Her hands explored his bare chest, that only had a small sprinkling of hair on it and she felt the taut muscles of his stomach. He was definitely fit, and she couldn't wait to see more of him.

Jake was surprised by the level of passion that Alexis was showing. She was taking control of the moment that he had been planning. He wasn't going to complain though because this proved that no matter what she said, she wanted him. The touch of her hands on his bare flesh made him shiver and he wanted desperately to feel her skin against his. He let his hands slide along her bare arms then caressed her back above her dress line. She was warm to the touch and he felt her shudder beneath his hands.

He broke their kiss and leaned forward to touch his lips to her bare shoulder. She smelled intoxicating and he wanted to see how she would taste. He gently grazed her skin with his tongue and he liked the way she tasted. Next he let his mouth wander to the strap of her dress and used his teeth to pull it down. He wanted to go slowly but his mind and body were urging him to go faster. It had been so long since he had been with a woman and he didn't want to ruin this moment. The decision the was taken out of his control though when she breathlessly whispered in his ear that she wanted him now then proceeded to nibble on his earlobe.

Jake groaned and stood up bringing her with him. Picking her up into his strong arms he carried her to the bed where he lay her down gently. He stood above her and looked at her with admiration, she was so beautiful. She grabbed him by the waistband and pulled him down to her, kissing him deeply. Her hands made quick work of his belt and zipper and he helped her take his pants off.

Alexis sat up and Jake pushed her dress up and over her head, tossing it on the floor behind him. She was wearing a sexy white lace bra and matching panties that nearly sent him over the edge just seeing her in them. He soon made quick work of her bra and it followed the same path that her dress had a moment ago. Sucking in a breath he admired her perfect breasts then lowered his head to suck on a pink nipple.

Jake felt Alexis shudder and she bit down on his shoulder. That only encouraged him to move on to the other breast and give it the same treatment he had just lavished upon the other one.

"Jake, I can't take anymore, I want you now!" Alexis cried out as he moved his hand down her leg

Being pushed almost to the edge he lifted his head and looked deeply into her eyes, searching. He saw what he was looking for, confirmation that this was really what she wanted. He shed his boxers and her panties in no time then he hovered above her, waiting for her final confirmation.

Alexis pulled him down to her and kissed him deeply while lifting her hips to him in an invitation to take her. Jake lowered himself and entered her slowly, he wanted to savour this moment. When he was fully in her he stopped and tried vainly to maintain control. She felt amazing and he knew he would not last long if he was not careful. He moved slowly within her and marveled at how she responded and moved with him. They moved in sync with each other and soon their lovemaking became frenzied. Neither of them held anything back and soon they were calling out the others name when their orgasm's over took them.

They lay in each others arms after, spent with exhaustion but reveling in what they had just shared. Alexis was lying on her side with Jake pressed up behind her and they fit together perfectly. Holding his hand, she kissed the back of it and pressed it to her chest. She was amazed at what they had just shared together, never having felt anything so intense before. She didn't have much experience with men, but she knew this was special. The question was, where did they go from here? It was something she didn't want to think about right now, later when she was alone she would revisit that question. For now, she wanted to enjoy the moment and bask in the warmth of Jakes embrace. She closed her eyes and drifted off in contentment.

Jake knew when Alexis fell asleep because he could feel her body relax against his and her breathing became slow and even. He held her close to him and wished that they could stay here forever. Today had turned out much differently than he had expected it to. Alexis had surprised him and not many people could do that to him. In three short day she had gone from insulting him to stealing his heart. Maybe Samantha was right, and Destiny was playing a part in their life. He thought about this as he drifted off to sleep as well.

Alexis awoke to feel Jake trailing kisses down her bare back and then back up. He snuggled back up behind her and kissed her neck eliciting a moan of pleasure from her. Jake buried his face into her silken hair and smiled. They spent the next half hour making love at a leisurely pace enjoying the pleasures they could give the other. Afterwards they once again fell asleep wrapped in one another's arms and stayed that way until the morning.

It was well past nine before they woke up and it was to the sound of Max barking outside the small cabins door. Alexis groaned and rolled over into Jake. She had awoken and forgotten that she was not alone. She opened her eyes to see Jake smiling at her and she smiled back shyly.

"Morning beautiful," Jake said pushing a stray hair off her face.

"Morning, what time is it?"

"A little after nine I think."

"Mmm. It's nice to sleep in, I don't do that very often."

"Neither do I, although I wish Max would shut up, he's ruining our quiet morning."

"Why's he being so noisy?"

"My guess is that he just came back from Marty and Susan's since they were supposed to be back sometime this morning."

"Awe, poor guy, should we let him in?"

"Not unless you want him here in bed with us."

"Umm, not really, I'd rather share my bed with just you."

"That I can deal with," Jake said just before he kissed her again.

Their kiss was slow and seductive and soon they were both aroused again, but before they could go any further they heard Becky calling Max's name.

"Oh my God, it's Becky. What will she think if she sees you stayed here last night?" Alexis cried out, scrambling out of bed and looking for her clothes.

"I'd say she'd be happy since we both know that her and Susan want us together," Jake laughed as he admired her naked body.

"Jake, be serious. We only just met, and we've already slept together. I know things have been moving fast for us but I'm not ready for your daughter to know that we spent the night together."

Jake sat up when he saw how serious Alexis was being and sighed. "I guess you're right, although she's a smart girl and I'm sure she will figure it out or at least know somethings happened. Not to mention I don't know if I'll be able to keep my hands off of you from now on."

With that he swiftly got out of bed and pulled her into his arms. She started to protest and gave up once her body came into contact with his bare flesh. All thought went out of her head until she looked over his shoulder.

"Jake, we can't do this, the curtains are still wide open, she could see us!" she exclaimed.

"Then let's make sure she doesn't, besides Susan or Marty will be with her and I'm sure they will make sure she doesn't come over here," he said as he let her go and went over to close the curtains, then he made sure the door was locked. Walking back to her, he took her by the hand and led her to the back of the cabin.

"Where are we going?"

"I think it's time to make our selves presentable so that means a shower first."

Alexis was shocked at first by this suggestion then she smiled and followed him. She had never showered with a man before, so this could be interesting.

Jake and Alexis arrived back at his cabin an hour later to find Becky and Marty watching cartoons on the television and Susan making pancakes in the kitchen.

"Good morning you two," Susan said with a knowing smile on her face.

"Morning Grandma," Alexis said, going to give her a kiss on the cheek.

"I take it you two had a pleasant night?"

"You could say that, but could we please talk about something else?"

"Whatever you want dear."

Alexis groaned and moved back around the island to sit on one of the bar stools. Jake was about to sit down when Becky came running over to give him a hug.

"Daddy! Where were you? You weren't here when we got back," she asked letting go of him, so she could look up at him.

"I got up early and asked Alexis if she wanted to go for a walk, we just got back," Jake said, hating that he had to lie to his daughter.

"Oh, okay. Maybe we could all go for one later Daddy?"

"Sure Sweat-Pea, I'd like that."

Becky smiled at her dad then went back to watch cartoons with her Grandpa Marty. Jake gave Alexis a wink then turned on his bar stool to talk to Susan. Ten minutes later they were all sitting around the big table eating pancakes with fresh fruit and coffee. It was a warm atmosphere and Alexis was content. It had been so long since she had felt like part of a family and today showed her everything she had been missing over the years.

After breakfast they all went on the walk that Jake had promised Becky then they went their separate ways. Alexis went to meet with the Stan, the contractor Jake had arranged to meet with her today, Marty and Susan took Becky to her swimming lessons and Jake went to finish some paperwork then went to run errands since it was his day off.

Alexis didn't have time to think over the events of the last twenty-four hours since she spent most of the afternoon going over her plans with the Stan. They went over the rough sketches she had made and also walked through The Inn going over some minor repairs and changes that needed to be made. By four o'clock Alexis was satisfied that everything had been covered and was impressed with Stan and knew he was the man for the job. He promised to have the surprise for her grandparents finished before the end of August, in time for their anniversary. He would start work on the inside of The Inn tomorrow and the construction outside would begin next week.

Now that she was done for the day, Alexis took her new book and walked into town, planning to sit in the park and read for a couple of hours before dinner. It was a beautiful day out and as she walked down the road towards the park as she took in the beauty of the small town and the surrounding mountains. She had always loved the mountains and as a child she had wished she lived here. Those dreams had been shattered her last summer here when she had vowed never to return. She thought about how silly she had been and regretted the missed time she could have had here in the town she had once loved, and the time she had missed with her grandparents.

You might also have met Jake earlier and never have met Frank, her inner mind said to her. She thought of that and wondered what her life might have been like if that were true. It was an interesting concept, but she didn't go any further with the idea. Instead she stopped in at Sam's to grab a coffee and say hi, but Samantha wasn't working today. Taking her coffee she made the short walk to the park and found an unoccupied grassy area under a tree and sat down to read her book.

Alexis immersed herself into the riveting story her book held, and she lost track of time as she usually did when she was reading. It wasn't until a dark shadow blocked the warmth of the sun that she paused in her reading to look up. She gasped in alarm when she saw who it was.

"What do you want?" she asked trying to move back but found herself up against the tree she was sitting under.

"Now that depends on what you're willing to give?" Ron answered with a suggestive leer.

"You're a pig, I see nothings changed over all these years, and you're drunk!" she spat.

"Now, now, no need to be insulting. I haven't done anything to deserve that, yet," he added.

Alexis looked around desperately to see if anyone was around. The area she was sitting in was empty of people and the ones further away would be of no help unless she screamed as loud as she could.

Ron saw her desperation and smiled coldly down at her. "You and I still have some unfinished business to take care of, and I believe I owe you one for what you did to me," he growled.

"What I did to you? What about what you did to me? You were supposed to be my friend and instead you tried to rape me!" She yelled at him, fury overtaking her fear.

"I don't see it that way. The way I saw it was that you were a city whore who wanted me, all you city girls are easy."

"I don't know why you thought that, but you were wrong, I was only sixteen and still a virgin."

"Now I really wish we hadn't been interrupted, I love virgins, they're the best to take."

"You're sick, you know that! No wonder why you spent time in jail. Who ever let you out should be shot because you deserve to rot in a cell by yourself!"

"Whoa, I see you've become quite feisty over the years. I think I'm going to really enjoy taking you when the time comes," Ron said looking over her body.

"It'll be a cold day in hell before you touch this body!"

Ron squatted down in front of her and saw the anger in her eyes, but also the fear from him being so close now. He grinned and grabbed her arm roughly, while the other hand made its way up her bare leg. "And who's going to stop me?" he whispered leaning over her.

Before she could answer he was jerked back roughly and thrown to the ground.

"Get off of her!" Alexis heard and saw Jake yell at Ron.

Ron scrambled to his feet and glared at Jake. "What's wrong Jake, don't like me talking to your woman?" he asked.

"That's not what I would call talking you bastard."

"What, we were just talking and picking up from where we left off all those years ago in the woods, weren't we darling?" Ron grinned down at Alexis.

Jake stepped in front of Alexis and balled his fists. "I should have done more than beat you into the ground all those years ago when I came across you and your goons that day. You're despicable and I'm going to make sure that this time you stay in jail where you belong."

"I'm not going back to jail, I ain't done nothing wrong."

"That's where you're wrong Ron, because you'll be interested to know that Brian and I went and had a talk with Mr. Webber today. It seems that your harassment and sexual misconduct here today with Alexis will be in breach of your parole."

At this Ron started to look worried and backed up a step. "You can't prove I did anything. She wanted me, and I'll tell everyone that. No one's going to believe that little bitch."

"I don't think that's going to work Ron."

"And why's that?"

"Take a look behind you, you idiot," Alexis yelled at him. She had gotten up and was standing partially behind Jake.

Ron turned to see people had been milling around listening to their conversation and coming down the path was Brian with the local law enforcement.

"It's over Jake. You're going to rot in jail and if they do ever let you out you'll never be welcome in this town again, because as we speak a petition is going around to have you banned from Silver Springs."

"You can't do that!" Ron yelled looking around nervously and looking for an escape.

"There's no where for you to go Ron. We're not alone and surrounded by your goons this time," Alexis called out.

Ron looked like a caged animal with no where to go. "You're going to pay for this Jake. You're always interfering. If it hadn't been for you that day in the woods I wouldn't have been distracted and gotten this little whore when I wanted to."

Ron lunged at Jake then and tried to take a swing at him. Jake easily blocked him and punched him in the gut. Ron dropped to the ground holding his stomach and threw every curse word he could think of at Jake. By then Brain was there and two of the police officers were hauling Ron to his feet and handcuffing him. When they were done, they started back down the path to where their patrol car was while the third officer stayed behind to question them.

"I'll kill you Jake, and that little bitch of yours," Ron yelled at them as he was taken away.

Jake ignored him and turned around to face Alexis. "Are you okay?" he asked looking her over.

"I am now, thanks to you," Alexis cried, throwing her arms around him.

She broke down into tears from the whole ordeal and clung to him. Jake wrapped his arms around her and held on tight. His heart broke for her and the pain she was feeling. He would do anything to take that pain away for her and to see her smile right now. But he knew that he needed to let her cry and get it out of her system. So he did the only thing he could do, which was to hold her and be there for her. He kissed the top of her head and waited until she had spent herself.

"I'm sorry," she murmured as she released him. I seem to always be crying on your shoulder and ruining your shirts."

"I don't mind, you can ruin as many of my shirts as you want," Jake replied, wiping the tears from her face then giving her a feather light kiss on her lips. "I just want you to be happy."

"I am now, thanks to you. I don't know what I would have done if you hadn't shown up when you did. I can't believe he would be brazen enough to try that out in the open."

"When it come's to Ron I'm not surprised but you don't have to worry about him again. He's going back to jail for a long time and Brian and I are working on making sure that he will never be allowed to set foot in Silver Springs again."

"I'm glad for that. By the way, how did you know I was here?"

"I didn't know you were here. Brian and I were at Mr. Webbers office and when we came out we saw Ron heading towards the park. He looked drunk and so we followed him to see what he was up to. I'm glad we decided to because I don't even want to think of what he might have done to you if we hadn't followed him. When we saw you off in the distance and Ron heading your way Brian went to get the police thinking Ron would do something when he saw you and I followed him. When I saw him talking to you I held back thinking maybe that's all intended to do, but as soon as he touched you I lost it and charged him. The thought of him touching you sickened me, and I wanted to kill him."

"Well I'm glad you came when you did," she said hugging him again.

"Me too," he said hoarsely.

"I'm sorry to interrupt Jake, but the officer would like to get a statement from Alexis if she's ready," Brian said from behind him.

"Sure. Are you okay to do this, because if not I can always bring you to the station later to give your statement," Jake asked looking at her in concern,

"I'm fine. Let me do this now so I can get it over with. I want to put all of this behind me and get on with my life. I feel like I'm finally getting closure for what happened all those years ago."

"I'm right here if you need me."

"Thank you, I appreciate it," she said giving him one of her special smiles then she went over to talk to the waiting officer.

"She's a strong one," Brian said in admiration.

"That she is. I'm amazed at how strong and resilient she is after everything she's gone through over the years," Jake replied.

"You've got good one there Jake, and I can see that she has feelings for you, even if she hasn't admitted it to you yet."

"I know."

"Okay, well then, I've already given my statement and the officer will need yours after Alexis. Are you okay if I leave because I'm sure word has spread, and Samantha will want to know what's happening."

"Sure, thanks for being here Brian. I owe you,"

"Anytime, now go take care of that young woman, she needs you."

"I will, for as long as she will let me."

Jake shook hands with Brian then went to stand with Alexis. Most of the crowd had dispersed except the few that stayed to give statements. Alexis finished telling the officer her story, which included what had happened when she was sixteen. Jake added to the statement on what he had witnessed and what he done. When they were finished they gathered up Alexis book that still lay on the ground then headed back to The Inn. Alexis was still shaken up a bit, but she was happy that this whole ordeal with Ron was finally over. It was a chapter in her life that she could put behind her now.

Chapter Twelve

It had been a long evening for Alexis and she climbed into her bed that night exhausted. She grandparents had been frantic, and she had spent a good portion of the evening reassuring them that she would be okay. They had wanted her to stay with them tonight, but she had told them she wanted to spend the night in her own bed. Jake had been worried about her and had asked her if she wanted him to stay the night and have Becky stay with her grandparents again. She had declined, wanting to have the night to herself and to get some much-needed sleep. He had respected her wishes and told her he would see her in the morning. Alexis was sleep almost as soon as her head hit the pillow.

The rest of the week passed by uneventfully and Alexis kept herself busy with the renovations. The carpenters had started refinishing the railing on the main staircase and the floors were being sanded and would be stained afterwards. Plans had been made with Jake to arrange the front reception area to be relocated while the floors were being done. Alexis had measured all the windows, and new curtains and drapes were being made by a local seamstress and they would be ready in two weeks. By the end of the week she was pleased with the progress of everything and felt like she was accomplishing the goal that her grandparents had given her. By Friday night she felt that she deserved a weekend to relax.

Alexis was unsure of what to do over the weekend since she had no plans and Jake and Becky had left for their camping trip that morning and wouldn't be back until Sunday night. She had finished her new book and decided that maybe a trip to Sam's would be the perfect thing to do and maybe stop to buy a bottle of wine to have later. The thought of having glass of wine while reading a good book sounded like the perfect way to unwind after a busy week.

Sam's was busy as usual, and Alexis made her way to the fiction isle to see if she could find something interesting to read. Looking around, she didn't see Samantha which was too bad since it would have been nice to chat with her new friend. She was reading the back of a book when a hand touched her arm to get her attention. She looked up to see Brian standing there looking down at her.

"Hi Brian," she said putting the book she was looking at back on the shelf.

"Hi Alexis, I saw you here and thought I would come over and say hi. I was surprised to find you in here alone, I thought Jake might be with you," he replied.

"No, it's just me. Jake and Becky are camping this weekend and won't be back until Sunday. Where's Samantha?"

"Knowing her, probably upstairs in her office. I was just coming by to get her to go meet some friends for dinner."

"That sounds nice, I hope you enjoy your night."

"You too, I'm sure we'll see you around here again soon."

Brian strode off towards the back of the store and Alexis wished she had what he and Samantha shared. Things were in the early stages with Jake and she wondered if one day they would be like those two. It was something that she would never have thought possible a week ago when her life was still in turmoil. She went back to browsing through a few more books before she made her selection and went to check out. She was just about to leave the store when she heard Samantha calling her name. She stopped and waited for the woman to reach her.

"Alexis, I'm so glad I caught you!" Samantha said when she stopped in front of her.

"What's up?" Alexis asked.

"What are you doing right now, I mean what are you're plans for tonight?"

"I'm not really sure. I had thought about maybe going to grab a bottle of wine and going home to read my new book, why?"

"If you don't have any plans I'd like you to join Brian and me tonight. We're going to meet with some friends for dinner up at the Silver Mountain Ski Resort and thought you might like to come. It would give you a chance to meet some more of the local residents, and friends of ours and Jakes."

"Oh, well I wouldn't want to impose since you already have these plans and I'm sure your friends won't want a complete stranger joining the group unannounced."

"Nonsense, you'll be welcomed. Any friend of Jakes is a friend of all of ours. Besides how would it look if we let you spend the night by yourself when you're new to town?"

"I don't know, are you sure they wouldn't mind?"

"Of course not, come on, we'll have a blast. Brian went to get my truck and will be waiting outside," she said ushering Alexis out the door.

True to her word, Brian was waiting in the truck just outside the store and the two women climbed in. Once they were buckled in Brian put the truck into gear and headed out of town. Alexis admired the view of the valley from the road that took them up the mountain side and was amazed by the size of the resort when it came into view. The main lodge was impressive and the sheer beauty of it took Alexis's breath away.

"This place has the same impression on everyone," Brian said from the front seat when he noticed the look on her face from the rear-view mirror. "I was the same way the first time I saw it."

"This place is amazing. I had heard people talking about it in town and now I can see why. The views from up here must be spectacular!"

"They are, just wait until you see the view from the restaurant where we'll be eating."

Brain parked the truck and the three of them climbed out and headed towards the beautiful front doors of the lodge. Once inside Alexis took in the main foyer and was in awe of the large stone fireplace. She would have to make sure to come up here in the wintertime and see this place during its peak season. She could just imagine a towering Christmas tree and a roaring fire for the skiers to come gather around after a day spent outside.

"Come on Alexis, this way," Samantha said as she linked her arm through hers and led her towards the restaurant. "Some of the others are already here," she added.

Alexis let Samantha lead her through the lodge to the restaurant where a hostess led them to their table.

"Stephen, Liz, I want you to meet Alexis, Marty and Susan's granddaughter," Samantha said introducing Alexis to the two people already sitting at the table.

"It's nice to meet you Alexis," they both answered, and Stephen stood up to pull her chair out for her.

"Why thank you," Alexis said sitting down in the chair,

"Your welcome," Stephen replied then sat back down beside his wife.

"I hope I'm not imposing, I mean Samantha was nice to invite me last minute and I hope it didn't put you out?"

"Not at all, we're happy to finally get a chance to meet you," Liz said waving her hand. "You're Marty and Susan's granddaughter so we already know so much about you, and now we get to finally meet the young lady behind the stories."

Alexis groaned at this and shook her head. "Is there anyone that those two haven't talked to about me?"

"If I know them as well as I do, I'd say probably not," Samantha answered with a laugh.

"Great."

"So, Alexis, how have you enjoyed being back in Silver Springs? We understand that it has been a long time since you were last here," Stephen asked her as he poured her a glass of wine.

"Honestly, it's been refreshing. I've forgotten just how much I've missed it here. The people I've met have been so friendly and I find it peaceful here. There have been a few incidents that I could have done without over the last week but that's the past now," Alexis answered truthfully.

"We heard about what happened with Ron, we're so sorry that you had to go through that. Thankfully he's gone now, and you will never have to deal with that lunatic again," Liz said with fervor.

"Yes, and I am grateful for that too. So, tell me, who else is joining us for dinner?"

"Our good friends Matt and Maggie will be joining us in a few minutes and I know you'll get along with them. While we're waiting why don't you tell us more about yourself, I'm sure what Marty and Susan have told all of us is only a small piece of who Alexis really is."

Alexis smiled at Liz and she knew she was going to like this woman. The evening passed by pleasantly with everyone sharing stories of growing up and how they had all met each other. Alexis was surprised to find out that Stephen and Liz were the owners of the Silver Mountain Ski Resort and that Stephen and Brian were in business together.

They talked for hours and the restaurant was closing when they finally all got up to call it a night. Alexis was happy that she had agreed to come with Brian and Samantha and hoped for many more nights like this in the future. Tonight, she had sat down and laughed and talked and was allowed to be her true self, unlike the past when she had had to be what others expected her to be. These people were real, and she knew that they would be true friends.

After saying good night, with promises to get together again soon, Brian, Samantha and Alexis headed home. They dropped her off in front of Jakes dark cabin and she walked around to hers. It seemed strange to see no lights on at Jakes, but she knew they would be back in two days.

They had not spent another night together since Sunday as they felt it wouldn't be right with Becky around. Instead they had stolen the occasional kiss at work and usually had lunch together at The Inn on their breaks. Alexis was content with the way things were going between her and Jake and felt that there was no need to rush into anything.

They had had an occasional argument over some of Alexis's choices for the décor but in the end, he would always relent and tell her that she would know best being the Interior Designer. The one area that he put his foot down on though, was his office. She was not to touch it because he liked it the way it was. Alexis had tried arguing with him, but she had eventually relented and left her plans for his office space alone.

Alexis smiled to herself as she thought of their arguments. They had left her feeling warm and aroused. She knew Jake had felt the same way by the looks he would give her afterwards. They were always at The Inn when this happened so neither of them had ever attempted to act upon their feelings afterwards.

Climbing into bed, Alexis thought of Jake and how good it would feel to be in his arms again.

The weeks passed by and by the end of July all the new renovations inside The Inn had been completed. The floors and new stairwell had turned out better than Alexis had hoped for and the new carpets and drapes in the bedrooms were installed. Painting had been finished the previous week and the restaurant had finished its make over as well. Alexis was proud of what she had accomplished and so were her grandparents. She had also kept the changes minimal to keep the original charm of the old building.

Outside two new docks were being built on the small lake, one for swimming and the other for the canoes and fishing. New flower beds were being added and would be completed by the end of the first week of August as well as some new hiking trails in behind The Inn. Alexis's surprise for her grandparents was still being built and she had decided not to have it brought over until the day before their anniversary.

Alexis and Jake were planning large anniversary party for the couple on their special day and were looking forward to helping them celebrate it. Fifty years was an incredible landmark and anyone who knew Susan and Marty knew that they were still very much in love. Alexis hoped to achieve the same thing as her grandparents one day, and she hoped that it would be with Jake.

Over the summer, her and Jake had grown a lot closer and were happy with how things were between them. They spent most of their free time together or with Becky, and more than anyone, Becky was the most delighted that her dad and Alexis were together. Alexis had grown very fond of the girl and treated her like she was her own daughter. She hoped one day to have her own daughter that was just like Becky, although a son would be nice too.

She didn't know what the future held for her and Jake, but she knew that she didn't want a future that didn't have him in it. Her heart was telling her that she loved him, but she had yet to say those words to him. She was afraid of what would happen after that since her last relationship had not gone well for her. Jake wasn't anything like Frank but her inner voice kept her from taking that step and letting Jake know how she felt. Alexis was fairly certain that he had the same feelings, but like her he had not said those words to her either and she wondered why. Maybe he was having reservations about telling her as well. She would just have to continue along the path they were on and see where it took them.

It was the first weekend of August and Alexis was deciding what else to pack when Becky came barging into her cabin without knocking. She looked up to see the girl smiling and out of breath.

"Aren't you packed yet? Daddy's waiting and I've been waiting forever!" she finally asked when she caught hr breath.

"Almost done, just trying to decide if there's anything else I need," Alexis answered.

Becky looked at the pile on the bed and started laughing. "We're only going camping for two nights, you don't need to bring everything with you."

"But I just want to make sure that I'm prepared for anything and if the weather gets bad."

"It's going to be warm all weekend and it's not supposed to rain, so grab half of what you have there and let's go! I'm dying to show you my favourite camping spot."

Alexis reassessed the pile and took some of the things and put them aside and then stuffed the rest into her backpack. Making sure everything was turned off, she left with Becky and locked the door behind her. She was excited for this trip since it would be the first time she had gone anywhere with both Jake and Becky, plus she had not been camping since she was a child. When Jake had asked her to join them she had been hesitant at first but after Becky pleading with her to come she had agreed.

Jake was waiting by the Jeep and he took her backpack from her when she walked up beside him.

"All ready to go rough it Lexi?" he asked.

Alexis warmed at the sound of him calling her by that nickname. Before it had been reserved for only her grandpa calling her that, but Jake had called her that one night in a moment of passion and he had continued calling her that.

"Ready as I'll ever be, it's been a long time since I've done this, and I hope I still like it," she said going around to get into the Jeep.

"Trust me, you'll love it. We have a few things planed that you enjoy."

"Okay, let's go then since I'm sure if we don't leave now Becky's never going to leave us alone."

"You should listen to her Daddy," Becky said from the back seat as she pet Max.

"Okay, Sweat-Pea, let's go show Lexi a weekend she'll remember forever."

Chapter Thirteen

Jake drove them through the town and down the highway to the south. They were heading for Silver Lake and it would take them about twenty minutes to drive there. The mountains towered above them on both sides of the valley with the highway following the Silver River. Jake pointed out some of the tourist areas and places where you could go white water rafting. Along the way they were treated to the sight of some mountain goats climbing the cliffs along the side of the road, and Jake stopped for a minute, so Alexis could watch them. She was amazed at how agile they were and the fact that they were not frightened of them, they just looked back at them curiously. They drove on and soon Jake was turning off onto a side road that would take them to where they were going to camp for the weekend.

After five minutes of traversing a rough road, Jake pulled up to a small clearing that overlooked Silver Lake. Alexis climbed out of the Jeep and walked towards the water, taking in the beauty around her. The clearing was grassy with wildflowers growing around it and in the center an area had been cleared with a firepit in it. She walked past a picnic table and down a slight incline to stop at a small gravel beach at the edge of the water.

The lake was calm today and the sun reflected off it's surface. The mountains surrounded them and across the lake she could see a beautiful lodge over looking the water. There were a few people out on the lake fishing and others exploring the shores. To their right down a ways, she could see a small camp ground filled with both tents and RV's. It looked like a nice spot, but she much preferred the one they were in.

"That's The Lodge at Silver Lake but everyone calls it The Lodge for some reason, kind of like The Inn," Jake said from behind her, nodding his head toward the lodge that she had been admiring a moment ago.

"It's beautiful, whoever owns that place is one lucky person," she replied.

"It's owned by an older couple, but they don't live there. They rent it out year- round to tourists who want to fish, a place to relax and occasionally as a honeymoon destination spot."

"It would be the prefect spot for the later."

"Yes, it would be," he said gathering her into his arms and resting his head beside hers.

They stood together like that looking out over the lake until Becky came running up to them breaking the silence surrounding them.

"Daddy come on. Let's get the tents set up so we can go for our hike then go fishing!" she said pulling his hand to drag him back towards the Jeep. Jake laughed and followed her with Alexis trailing along behind them.

When they had finished setting up camp they took a trail that left their clearing and headed into the surrounding forest. Alexis could tell that the trail was used often as it was well worn and there was the occasional sign of human use. The path followed a small creek the was coming down from the mountains and they hiked beside it up into the hills and Alexis soon found that she was not in the shape she used to. Breathing heavily, she tried to keep up but after a few more minutes asked if they could stop for a break.

Becky gave a little huff of exasperation but relented and waited beside Alexis who had sat down on a fallen log. Jake came to stand beside them and offered Alexis a water bottle which she gratefully accepted. After taking a long drink she handed it back and tried to regulate her breathing.

"So how much farther is it to where were going," Alexis eventually asked.

"About five more minutes. We can stay here for a bit though if you want to stop for a little longer," Jake answered taking a drink from the bottle.

"No, I'm good, lets go. I thought I was in better shape, but theses hills are killing me. At least on the way back it'll be all down hill."

"Yes, there is that," Jake laughed as he gave her his hand to help her up.

Becky took off down the path ahead of them with Max and left the two of them alone. They walked slowly holding hands and enjoyed the solitude around them. The birds were chirping and occasionally they saw a rabbit bound across their path. Alexis loved this place and was happy that she had agreed to come along. The path they were on was currently going through a dense part of the forest and Becky was no where to be seen.

"Are you sure Becky is okay since we can't see her?" she asked Jake.

"She'll be fine. I've been bringing her here for years and she knows this trail better than anyone, plus Max is with her," Jake added.

"Okay. If you say so."

"Don't worry, we're just about there. It's just around the bend in the path up there, Becky's probably waiting for us impatiently."

They kept walking and when they went around the bend Jake had pointed out, Alexis stopped in her tracks. Hidden within the forest was a glen with an old cabin and a pond fed by the stream they had been following. Wild flowers bloomed everywhere in a riot of colours and Max could be seen in the distance chasing something.

"This place is breath taking," Alexis breathed. Who would have known that this place could exist with all the forest surrounding it? "How did you ever find this place?"

"It belonged to my family and now it's mine, although as you can see it's not used anymore," Jake answered.

"Why would you not want to use a place as amazing as this?" she asked as she turned to take it all in.

"I had planned to someday renovate this place but then I had Becky and I never got around to it. I still hope to one day fix the place up as a weekend getaway, and to leave to Becky one day."

"That sounds nice, I think you should do it. This would make an amazing place to get away to on the weekends or even to rent out."

"I never thought if that, but I guess it would be perfect for that. I'd probably have to bring power and water up to it though to do that."

"Why? Why not make it an off the grid cabin? Bring in some solar panels for energy and I'm sure you could get your water from the stream."

"You know, that's a great idea. I don't know why I never thought of that. Maybe I'll have to tackle this project with you at my side for help."

"I'd like that, we could have fun doing this together."

"Now you've got me all excited about this place, a feeling I haven't had here since I was a kid. Wait until I tell Becky about this!"

"Tell me about what Daddy?" Becky asked walking around the corner of the cabin to where they were.

"We were just talking about renovating this place and making it usable again Sweat-Pea," Jake answered his daughter.

"That would be amazing Daddy! Then we could camp here instead."

"Yes, I guess we could do that too."

"When can we start? Could we start right away? I'd like to help too!"

"Whoa, hang on Seat-Pea. We would still have to make up plans, see about permits and I'd have to find time in-between work to do this before we could start. Right now, it's just an idea."

"Oh, okay," Becky said sadly and looked at the ground.

Jake lifted her chin to looks at her sad face. "Don't worry, we'll do it just as soon as we can. Besides, we're here to have fun this weekend and to show Lexi all our favourite things to do while camping."

"Okay Daddy," Becky said putting on a smile. "Come on Miss Alexis, I want to show you the pond!" she said excitedly.

Alexis smiled down at the little girl who waited for her and she couldn't help but admire the resilience she had. One minute she was heart broken then the next excited. She took the girl by the hand and let herself be led off by Becky. The pond was crystal clear and the clouds in the sky above were reflected across its surface. It was not a deep pond and it was only bout thirty feet across. They explored the edges of the water and watched the water bugs skimming across the waters surface and the occasion frog leapt out of the grass and into the pond. When one of the frogs did this, Max would try and catch it and on more than one occasion he landed in the pond as well. Becky thought this was hilarious and the sound of her laughter echoed through the small glen.

They spent a good part of the afternoon there, before Jake announced that it was time for them to leave as it was a long hike back. Becky didn't want to go but as soon as her dad reminded her about fishing she was off down the path with Max following.

"I don't know how she has so much energy," Alexis said to Jake as they followed at a slower pace.

"She's always been like this, full of energy and high spirited. It's one of the things I love about her," Jake responded. "Most kids these days are only interested in their computers and cellphones, instead of enjoying what nature has to offer. Becky on the other hand is the opposite, she loves to spend most of her time outdoors."

"That's true, I couldn't imagine growing up the way most kids do these days."

They walked on silently after that and every once in awhile they would see Becky and Max down the trail as she waited for them to catch up. They were nearing the camp, when Jake grabbed her hand and stopped her. He pulled her to him and kissed her passionately. Alexis immediately responded to him and heat rose throughout her body as he pressed his body closer to him. She ran her fingers through his hair and urged him to keep kissing her when he was about to pull back. He obliged and soon her knees were weak from their passion for each other.

"Lexi, I want you so much," Jake breathed into her ear when he finally broke away from her swollen lips. "It feels like it's been forever."

"I know Jake, I want you to, but we can't, Becky is waiting for us," she responded weakly. "We'll have to wait until we get back to town."

"I don't know if I can last that long, knowing that you will be in the tent next to me."

"We have to, we can't do this with your daughter here, it would be wrong."

"I know, but I don't know how I'm going to mange to keep my hands off of you this weekend."

"You'll just have to try. Think of it this way, waiting will just make it that much better when we do finally get to be together."

Jake groaned at the thought of having to wait and Alexis could feel just how much he wanted her since he was still pressed up against her. He hugged her tightly then let her go so they could make their way back to their camp site. Jake walked awkwardly for the first minute and Alexis tried not notice the bulge in the front of his pants but couldn't resist taking a look. Jake noticed this and gave her a warning look and she turned her head quickly to look at a butterfly. She heard him groan again and she tried not to laugh at his at his misery, besides she was feeling the same way, it just wasn't visible. They arrived at the camp to find Becky playing fetch with Max and as soon as she saw them she ran to get the fishing poles.

"What took you two so long?" Becky asked.

"Lexi was admiring a butterfly," Jake answered with a smirk.

"Oh, okay. Come on Daddy lets get the bait and go fishing before dinner. Did you remember to bring an extra rod for Miss Alexis?"

"Yes. How about it Lexi? Are you up for some fishing?"

"I'm game but I'm probably no good at it anymore," Alexis said with a laugh.

"Don't worry, not the greatest at it either, it's just for fun," Becky said with a grin.

"Okay, then let's go see if we can catch some fish." Having said that Alexis headed for the water with Jake bringing all the gear and bait.

An hour later they returned to start a fire and get dinner ready. Fishing had been fun with Becky catching the largest fish. They had been fishing on the catch and release policy as Becky didn't like to keep them and Alexis was glad for that since she felt the same way and did not relish the idea of having to clean them.

While cooking their burgers and hotdogs over the fire, they talked about everything they had seen and did that day and as they were eating talk returned to restoring the old cabin. Jake told Alexis about how his grandfather had built the cabin for hunting and when he had passed away it had been left to his father. Jakes father had taken him camping there when he was a child but when he got older he was no longer interested in going there anymore, so it had been abandoned. Now it would take a lot of time and effort to restore it. Becky was excited about what they could do with it and soon all three of them were caught up in the plans to restore the old cabin.

They stayed up late sitting around the campfire roasting marshmallows and telling scary campfire stories. By ten Becky was asleep in her chair, so Jake picked up the little girl and put her to bed in the tent that they shared. When she was tucked in he came back out and took Alexis by her hand and pulled her up out of her chair and into his arms.

"I've been wanting to do that all night," he said as he rested his chin on her head.

"Me too. You're nice and warm," Alexis added.

Jake hugged her closer to share his warmth and they stood there quietly with the fire crackling and throwing off heat. Jake released her after a bit and led her down towards the water.

"I love it out here," Alexis sighed as they stood there looking out over the lake.

"It's so peaceful. I used to come here a lot by myself when I needed to get away from everything and clear my head. It's a good place to just relax and find yourself," Jake said looking up at the stars in a cloudless night sky.

"I can see why you would do that. I wish I'd had a place like this to go to over the years. In the city there aren't really many places go where you can find some peace and quiet. You had to go out of the city to find that."

"Do you miss the city?"

"I thought I would but no, I don't miss the city. I couldn't imagine living anywhere else now. I've grown to love Silver Springs again and the people here."

"And does that include me?" Jake asked quietly

Alexis turned to him to see him watching her closely. She knew what he was asking, and it was her opportunity to finally tell him how she felt. She thought about it for a moment before deciding to take the leap and see what happened

"Yes. I'm in love with you Jake," she answered.

Jakes whole face lit up with those four words and he pulled her into his arms again and kissed her deeply. When he finally released her mouth, he looked deeply into her eyes and said, "I love you too Lexi."

Alexis's heart skipped a beat as he declared his love for her and tears gathered in her eyes. She had never felt this happy in her entire life and she never wanted this moment to end. She had taken the chance in telling him how she felt, and he had not disappointed her. She had been right, he did love too. Alexis kissed him while thinking that this would be a camping trip she would definitely never forget, just as Jake had promised.

The rest of the weekend passed with them swimming in the very cold lake, hiking along new trails and fishing. They spent the night around the campfire and anyone observing them would think they were a family, as they looked and acted like one. Becky loved spending time with Alexis and she lit up whenever she was near. Alexis was proud of the little girl and she loved her like she was her own.

Alexis marveled at how different her life was from two months ago. Never would she have thought that she would be here with a man that loved her and a little girl that thought the world of her. Had she stayed in the city and never moved here, she would never have known these joys in life. Her trepidation of moving here had long since past and she now looked forward to her life here. Jake and Becky had made it possible for her to see how much better life could be if you lived it the way you wanted to and not the way others thought you should. She would be forever grateful to the two of them for this and she would do everything she could to make them happy.

Chapter Fourteen

The following week passed in a blur and by the weekend most of the renovations outside were done. The surprise gift for Marty and Susan that Alexis had had included in the renovations was coming along nicely and she couldn't wait for her grandparents to see it on their anniversary.

Now that everything was close to being finished, Alexis wasn't sure what to do. She had been hired by her grandparents to renovate The Inn, but she had never thought about what she would do after that. She would have ask around and see if there were any jobs available or perhaps open her own business here. However, to do that she would have to have money and that was something she was lacking because of Frank. The thought was depressing but there was nothing she could do about it right now except explore other possibilities.

On Saturday she spent the afternoon in town to work out some details for her grandparent's anniversary party and then went to meet Samantha for coffee. Afterwards her and Samantha would met up with the guys and head over to Stephen and Liz's place for a barbeque. Alexis was speechless when she saw their cabin and it made Jakes seem small in comparison. The views were spectacular from here and Alexis could see why Stephen had chosen this spot to build his home, she would have done the same.

Stephen and an obviously pregnant Liz had set up the picnic table out back with drinks and lots of delicious snacks for all of them. They played several lawn games with the women against the men, in which the men lost badly but with some grace. Afterwards they sat around the fire pit while Stephen grilled their steaks to perfection and then dinner was eaten around the fire.

Alexis was happy, and she thought herself extremely lucky to have friends like this in her life. She was sitting on Jake's lap, snuggling against him when Liz brought up the question everyone had been dying to ask them but hadn't.

"So, should we be planning a wedding for you two soon?" Liz asked candidly.

Jake turned red and Alexis wasn't sure what to say.

"I told you Destiny had plans for both of you and I was right. Look at the two of you, you're perfect for each other," Samantha added.

"Umm, I don't know, it's not something we've talked about," Alexis finally answered.

"Oh, I thought maybe you had. I'm sorry, I didn't mean to make you uncomfortable," Liz said as she rubbed the small bulge in her stomach.

"It's alright. I mean Jake and I are still in the early stages of our relationship and enjoying our new-found love. I guess when we're ready to talk about it we will, right Jake?" Alexis asked the last turning on his lap to look at him.

"You can count on it," he said with a smile.

"Okay Liz, lets leave these too love birds alone and let's talk about something else," Stephen teased.

"Oh, alright. So Alexis, now that you're almost finished The Inn what are your plans?" Liz asked.

"I'm not sure. I would love to open up my own business, but I think it might be to early to do that, so I'll probably just look to see if there are any jobs available in town right now," Alexis answered.

"I'm sure Brain and Stephen could find you a job, isn't that right hon?" Liz said nudging her husband.

"I think that's a good possibility," Stephen said looking to Brian. "We're building a new ski chalet with guest rooms and amenities that will be done next year. We would be happy to hire you as our interior designer for that. Plus I'm sure we could find some other jobs for you to do in the meantime. I still have some things I would like to do to some of the older cabins at the ski hill and the main lodge. That is if you're interested in doing something like that."

"Interested? I would love to take on a project like that! I don't know how I can ever repay you for your kindness," Alexis said, tears coming unbidden to her eyes.

"No thanks are needed, the fact that you've made Jake a happy man is all we care about," Brian replied.

"You guys are all amazing, I am truly lucky to have met you all and that you have made me a part of your group."

"And we are happy to have you as part of our group," Samantha said with a warm smile and leaned over to squeeze her hand.

Jake shifted and wrapped his arms around her holding her close and leaned in to whisper in her ear. "You're one of us now Lexi."

"I can live with that," she whispered back. "I love you," she added.

"And I love you too," he answered and kissed gently on the lips.

"Alright you two, take it inside would you, we don't need to see that!" Brian teased.

"Oh Brian, leave them alone," Samantha chided as she leaned over and gave him a kiss before he could say anything else.

Everyone laughed at this and they continued to talk and drink Bailey's late into the night. It had been agreed that they would all stay the night as Stephen didn't want anyone drinking and driving so when they all decided to call it a night they headed to their rooms. This would be the first time that Jake and Alexis had spent a night alone together since that first time in her cabin over a month ago. They had managed to spend some time together when Becky was not home, but it had not been very often. So spending tonight together instead of having to sneak in a few hours here and there was going to be a rare treat.

Once in their room, they wasted no time and quickly shed their clothes while passionately kissing each other and trying to touch each other everywhere. They never made it to the bed but landed on the soft carpet where they made love with no reservations and both quickly succumbed to intense orgasms. They lay there wrapped in each other arms gasping for breath afterwards and enjoyed their closeness.

"That was amazing," Alexis stated when she had finally controlled her breathing.

"Definitely, although I had been planning on taking you slowly and savouring every minute of it," Jake replied.

"There's nothing saying you still can't do that," Alexis said as she ran her hand across his bare chest.

"Very true, besides we have all night and I plan to use every minute of it on you."

"I'm going to hold you to that, but first I think I have some plans of my own."

"Oh, and what would that be?"

"Why don't you just lay back and I'll show you."

"If you insist," Jake answered as he watched her climb on top of him.

Alexis felt emboldened and let herself explore Jakes body with no hesitation. Never in her life had she ever felt this free to act as she wished in the bedroom and it was an intoxicating feeling. She felt so alive with Jake and everything felt right with him. She felt things she had never felt before and tonight she planned to show him just what that did to her.

They spent most of the night making love and talking quietly of their dreams. It was quite late in the morning before either of them awoke and even then, they didn't get up before making love to each other one last time before they showered and went down to meet the others.

When they arrived downstairs the others were sitting out on the balcony having coffee and Brian and Stephen gave them big grins when they sat down. Alexis blushed slightly but warm smiles from the Samantha and Liz made her relax.

"I'm famished," Alexis said leaning over to pick up a strawberry from they tray of fresh fruit.

Everyone burst out laughing at that and that caused Alexis to blush again as she realized what she had said and what it had implied.

"You guys are impossible!" she said in exasperation as she popped the strawberry into her mouth.

After everyone had finished their coffees and eaten the fruit, they said their goodbyes and headed home. Jake had driven this time, so he headed towards Brain and Samantha's home. Alexis had never seen their place before and fell in love with their home as soon as she saw it. It was peaceful there and it overlooked Silver Creek.

Samantha invited them to stay for a while so Jake called Susan and Marty to see if they could watch Becky for the afternoon, to which they happily agreed to. Samantha showed Alexis around and explained to her that the cabin had once belonged to Brian's brother Keith and that he was the one who had had it built. She was also surprised to learn that Keith had left the cabin to Samantha in his will and not Brian. Samantha went on to tell her their story as Brian and Jake went out back to look at something.

"You two have such an amazing story," Alexis said when Samantha finished telling it.

"Yes, we do. Although it saddens me to have lost my best friend, it's what brought Brian and me back together," Samantha replied. "So tell me, now that we're alone, just how serious is it between you and Jake?"

"I don't know to be honest. I mean, we love each other and are happy but we haven't really talked about the future and what it might hold for us. So far we've just been living in the moment and not looking any further."

"Do you see a future with him?"

"Yes. I couldn't imagine my life without him now."

"Well that's good to hear. Jake's a good guy, you'll never meet anyone with a bigger heart than his. For him to have come out of a self-proclaimed bachelorhood for you means that he see's something in you that he's been looking for. It was something that we were all beginning to think he would never do. I still think Destiny had something to do with the two of you."

"I'm flattered that I was the one he was waiting for and in a sense, I feel the same way about him. Everything that has happened to me over the past years has brought me here. If not for those things I may never have come back and met him and fallen in love with him. So maybe there is something to this belief of yours, that Destiny or Fate has played a role in our coming together."

"Well I for one am glad that it happened. Not just for Jake but for Becky too. I have never seen her so happy and alive. She's wanted nothing more than to have a mother and she see's you in that role. I know it's a scary thing to have thrust upon you, but do you see yourself in that role? I mean, I'm only asking because I don't want to see Becky get hurt in any way."

"I understand what you're getting at, and I would be cautious too if I were you. But I've grown to love Becky as if she were my own and no matter what happens between Jake and myself I will always be here for her. Although I must admit that I hope that one day Jake will ask me to marry him and then I can be everything she needs."

"Give him time. I sure he wants to but is waiting for the right moment. For now enjoy your time together. Now tell me, are you up for going swimming?"

"Swimming, where? Plus I don't have a swim suit with me."

"Not to worry, you're close to the same size as me, so I have one you can borrow, and as for where, well you'll jus have to wait and see. Are you game?"

"Sure, I mean if Jake wants to and doesn't need to get back."

"Oh trust me, I'm sure he'll want you to see this place. Come on, lets go see what the guys are up to and see if they want to go."

The two women went out to the back of the cabin where the guys were looking over Brian's new ATV. It was a bright red and still shiny. When they saw the women approach they stopped talking and greeted them.

"I asked Alexis if she wanted to go swimming. Are you two up for that?" Samantha asked sliding up next to Brian.

"I am, plus I can show Jake what this thing can do on the way," Brian answered and nodded to the ATV they were just looking at. "What do you say Jake?"

"I'm game if you guys don't have anything else you need to do," Brian replied.

"Nope, we were just going to go for a ride later with the ATV's. Come on, I think you left your swim suit here the last time you were over."

With that decided, they all headed back into the cabin and Samantha found a swim suit that Alexis could wear. She put it on under her shorts and t-shirt, then went to help Samantha pack a basket with wine, cheese, fruit, sandwiches and some bottled water. They figured they might as well make the most of it and have a picnic while they were there too. Once that was done they took everything outside where they guys had Brian's new ATV and Samantha's older one waiting.

Brain and Jake took off in the new one and Samantha and Alexis followed them at a slower pace. They had shouted at them not to break their necks before they left but weren't sure if they had heard them. Laughing the two women watched their guys disappear into the forest and then chatted idly about whatever topic came up. It didn't take them long to get to where they were going and when Samantha stopped her ATV at the edge of the meadow, Alexis was once again surprised at the hidden beauty to be found in the woods surrounding Silver Springs.

This one was unique in comparison to the other places she had seen. Not only was there a meadow filled with wildflowers, but a waterfall thundered down into a large pond and then Silver Creek continued its way through the forest and out of sight. Alexis turned in circles taking it all in and breathed in the fresh air.

"I told you would love it here. It's my favourite place in the world, there's no where else I'd rather be than here," Samantha said walking through the tall grass with Alexis.

"I can see why," sighed Alexis as they walked towards the pond. "What is this place?"

"It's called Silver Creek Falls. It's a popular place around here. Brain and I own the land it's on, but we let the locals come here as well as long as they respect and maintain the wildlife here."

"That's very generous of you to do that."

"Yes well, we figured that it's too nice a place to keep to just ourselves. Plus when we were teenagers, Brian and I used to come here, and this is where we first fell in love with each other. It has a special meaning to us and we hope that others may find the same thing as we did here."

"That's such a heartwarming story and reason to let others come here. I can see why this place is so special to you two."

"It's not just that, this was also Keith's favourite spot. Earlier this year, Brian and I spread his ashes here and we feel like his spirit is here in the place he loved the most. It's like he's always with us here."

"Oh Samantha, that's so beautiful and I can see why you and Brian cherish this place so much."

"Come on, let me show you around then we'll go get the wine. We might as well have a drink while we wait for the guys, I imagine they won't get here for a few more minutes if I know them."

"Sure, I'm up for that."

Samantha showed her around the meadow and pond then they went back to the ATV where they took the picnic basket back to a table by the waters edge. They spread a checkered cloth over the table then laid the food and drinks out. Once done they poured themselves a glass of wine then sat down on the grass to wait for the guys to arrive.

Alexis and Samantha were deep in conversation when Jake and Brain arrived, and they laughed at the sight of them. They were covered in mud and their hair was sticking up when they took their helmets off.

"What did you guys do, find every mud muddle you could find?" Samantha asked.

The two men looked guilty and it was Brian who answered. "Not every single one."

Samantha laughed and then cried out when Brian gave her a big muddy hug and kiss. Jake looked to do the same to Alexis, but her look stopped him.

"I'm hungry, what's for lunch?" Jake asked instead.

"No way, you are not coming near the food until you both go jump in the pond and clean off," Samantha stated with a stern look.

"Brain, your wife is a tyrant," Jake said with a groan.

"Tell me about it," Brian answered, only to earn himself a glare from Samantha. "But we better do as she says, or we'll never hear the end of it."

Samantha was about to comment on that, but Brian took off and jumped in the pond fully clothed. Jake followed soon after. Samantha rolled her eyes and muttered, "men"!

Once clean they came back minus their wet clothes and wearing only their swim suits. Samantha and Alexis were also wearing only their swim suits and were laying on towels sun tanning when they arrived. Jake dropped down to lay beside Alexis who looked sexy as hell in what she was wearing.

"Jake you're freezing!" she screamed trying to roll away from him.

Jake laughed and caught her and wrapped his arms around her. "Then you should warm me up," he said with a heated look.

Alexis knew that look and her body instantly reacted to him. "Not here with our friends," she whispered.

"Okay but I intend to have my way with you at the first opportunity I can get."

"You promise?"

"Yes."

Alexis gave him a heated look back and wished desperately that they were alone right now, so Jake could do what he wanted to her.

"If you keep looking at me like that I'm not going to be able to wait and our friends are going to get a show," Jake growled in her ear.

Alexis was close to letting him, but her modesty got the better of her and she stood up quickly to put some space between them.

Jake looked up at her and Alexis's knees quivered when she saw the look of desire aimed at her.

"I think maybe we should have something to eat," she said in a shaky voice.

Jake got up and kissed her. "Food is not what I'm hungry for right now."

"Jake, please, not here in front of the others."

"Fine, you win this round, but I'll be coming for what I want soon," he said with a smile as he let her go and headed over to the table.

Alexis let out a deep sigh of relief and followed him. Thankfully Brain and Samantha were a sitting about twenty feet away with their backs to them and had not heard or seen their exchange.

A few minutes later they joined them, and they ate a light lunch then relaxed in the sun for a bit before they went swimming. The pond was freezing, but like the lake at The Inn it became bearable as long as you kept moving. When they finally tired and got cold they climbed out and Jake offered to show Alexis the area around the falls and the view from the top.

She followed him along the path with her towel wrapped around her and he helped her up some of the steeper parts of the trail by the side of the falls. Once up there Alexis gazed at the view below them and blushed when she saw Brian kissing Samantha and turned away feeling like she was intruding on their privacy.

"Remember, they're still newly weds," Jake told her when he saw where she had been looking.

"I know, so let's give them some privacy and go for a hike if that's alright with you?"

"Sure. Come on there a place up here I think you would like."

He took her hand and they walked together along the path that followed the creek. A short distance away they stopped at an area where the creek had made a shallow pool.

"This is a beautiful little spot," Alexis stated.

"Not as beautiful as you are right now," Jake responded before he kissed her.

Alexis kissed him back and soon the passion they had been fighting earlier came to a boil. They couldn't stop, and Jake laid her down on the small patch of grass and then removed her swim suit. He then covered every inch of her body in kisses and Alexis groaned in sheer pleasure. She cried out as he stopped in one spot and brought her to an earth-shattering climax. When she finally recovered from it, Jake was lying beside her watching her.

"I've been wanting to do that to you ever since I saw you in that skimpy bikini you call a swim suit," Jake said as he looked over her naked body.

"Well, I'm glad we went for this hike then," Alexis quipped.

"Oh, I'm not done yet."

"What do you mean by that?

"Come on I'll show you what I mean."

He pulled her up then took his suit off and jumped into the small pool.

"Jake are you crazy," she shouted standing there naked.

"Nope, now come in or I'm coming out to get you!"

Knowing that he would do just that, she jumped in and joined him. Jake went over to her and nibbled on her ear then kissed her neck. Picking her up he wrapped her legs around him and before she knew what was happening he was thrusting himself into her. She shuddered as he entered her so soon after her recent climax and immediately started to move with him. She kissed him passionately and they made love to each other in that small pond above the waterfalls. Afterwards, they swam around for awhile before they decided they should go join Brain and Samantha again. They left the small pool with intentions of coming back again before it got too cold.

Alexis was filled with happiness and she knew in her heart that Jake would be the one she would marry and spend the rest of her life with.

Chapter Fifteen

Alexis met with Brian and Stephen on the following Wednesday to go over the plans for the new lodge and she pitched some ideas on how she thought it could be decorated. Her ideas were modern mixed with rustic to compliment the surrounding area and both men were impressed with her suggestions. Since the new lodge would not be finished until the following year she would still need to find a job in the meantime. Brian helped her out with that, saying that he would like to have the offices he had bought in town earlier this year redone. Alexis was grateful for the job and it was agreed that she would start in September after her grandparent's anniversary. Until then she would have to find something to keep her occupied since there wasn't much she could do to help with the few outdoor renovations left at The Inn.

On Thursday Jake came to her saying he had taken the day off and asked her if she wanted to join him for the day. Becky was staying with a friend, so he was going to drive up to the old cabin to see what he would need to start the renovations. Ever since their camping trip Becky had done nothing but talk about it and had pestered her dad until he had finally relented and agreed to start the project as soon as possible. He had always had a hard time saying no to her.

Alexis agreed to go with him, so they packed a lunch and some blankets, along with a broom and some cleaning supplies to take with them to the cabin. She was glad for Jakes Jeep when he turned off onto the dirt trail that would take them to his cabin in the woods. The road was very bumpy and if it hadn't been for her seatbelt she probably would have landed in Jake's lap, not that she would have minded. The trail ended at the edge of the woods and Alexis thought the place was even more beautiful than the last time she had seen it. She climbed out of the Jeep and went around to stand beside Jake.

"You have your own little piece of paradise here. You're truly lucky to be able to own a place like this," she said to him.

"I realize that now, because when I was younger I never really appreciated this place. I'm glad I didn't sell it when I inherited it like I was going to," he told her.

"Really, you were going to sell it?"

"Yes, but something always stopped me from doing it and I'm not sure why. But now I see that it will be a great place for Becky to come to like I did as a kid and her kids in the future." Jake sounded wistful as he said this, and Alexis looked at him to see him smiling.

"Come on, lets go take a look and see if we can make all that happen for her."

The two of them walked to the cabin hand in hand and Jake unlocked the door when they reached it. Inside it was one big room with two smaller rooms off the back that were bedrooms. There was no indoor plumbing or electrical as it had been meant to be a rustic hunting cabin. Jake opened all the shutters to let the light in and they inspected the cabin to see what needed to be fixed or replaced. They were surprised to find it in better shape than they were expecting it to be in. Apparently when Jake's grandfather had built it, he had built it to last.

"For it's age and disuse it's in surprisingly good condition," Alexis commented.

"I agree. It looks like all we really need to do is replace a couple of floor boards, replace the kitchen counter, buy new mattresses and curtains and give the place a good scrub. That should be easy to do and should take no time at all. Although I think adding a small addition to the back for a washroom would be in order. I don't relish the idea of having to use an outhouse, even it this place is supposed to be rustic.'

"I'm with you on that one. What are you thinking, a septic tank with a flush toilet or a composting toilet?"

"I think if I decided to rent this place out I'd go with getting running water into here and a septic tank. Not to mention I don't think that Becky would go for that rustic of a cabin."

"Okay so, if you decide to go that way, how much time do you think it would take to get this place done?"

"I'm not sure. Stan owes me a few favours and could get him to do the work which wouldn't take long but the septic tank and running water might take awhile. I think I'll go outside and give him a call and see what he has to say, and how much it will cost me."

"Okay, I'll go the cleaning supplies from the Jeep and bring them in."

While Jake was on the phone with Stan, Alexis brought everything in then started sweeping years of dirt out the cabin door.

By the time Jake came back in she was done the sweeping and was sneezing uncontrollably. Jake laughed when he saw her, and she looked at him in confusion.

"You're a mess, you're covered in dust and your hair is sticking out wildly," he explained.

"Well you do what I just did and see what you like afterwards," she said swatting the broom at him.

Jake laughed again and easily avoided the broom and caught her. He wiped some dirt off her face and then leaned down to kiss her. She dropped the broom and wrapped her arms around him and returned the kiss. After, he took her by the hand and led her outside.

"Where are we going?" she asked.

"Going to get you cleaned up," he answered as he grabbed the blankets off the chairs that Alexis had put outside before she had started sweeping.

"And where am I supposed to get cleaned up?"

"Why in the pond of course, where else would I take you?"

"But it's cold and I don't have any towels."

"Don't worry, I'll keep you warm." He gave her a look that implied what it meant.

"Oh," was all she could say.

Jake stopped at the edge of the pond and laid one of the blankets out on the grass. Next, he slowly removed all of her clothes until she was standing naked before him. She shuddered at the look he gave her, and she wanted him. She undressed him, and they lay down on the blanket to explore each other's bodies. They were in no rush and slowly pleased one another and then made love in the warm sun until they were spent. Afterwards they lay curled up together and fell asleep.

When they awoke they made their way into the cold pond, so Alexis could finally clean off and then swam around to keep warm. Jake was the one to splash her first which ended in a fierce water battle which neither of them won. Instead they ended up in each others arms and made love again.

Later, when they had dried off and redressed, they ate their lunch outside then tackled the cleaning inside the cabin. They were proud of what they had achieved in one day and when they left, the place was ready to start work on. While they had been cleaning, Jake had filled Alexis in on what Stan had to say. Since he had a large crew this year he had the manpower to start work on the cabin on Saturday and would have the permits ready by the middle of the following week to start the excavation to install as septic tank and to run a water line from the creek to the cabin. Stan would also put in the order for solar panels and batteries right away. He figured it would take him about three to four weeks to finish everything if the weather stayed nice. Alexis was surprised at how quickly things could get done here. In the city it could take months just to start a project like this.

Alexis was happy for Jake and she knew Becky would be ecstatic when she heard the news. When they returned home, Alexis went to shower as she was to meet her grandparents for dinner and Jake went to pick up Becky from her friend's house. It had been a wonderful day and she went to meet her grandparents feeling like she was on cloud nine.

Dinner was pleasant, and her grandma was beaming with joy because her granddaughter was in love with Jake. She had known the two of them would be perfect for each other and was counting the days until they announced their engagement. She hoped it would be soon because it would tie into the surprise that her and Marty were dying to tell them in two weeks. She was bursting to tell them now, but Marty made her see the logic in waiting until the moment was right, which was not right now.

After dinner, the three of them walked through town from the restaurant they had just dinned in when Alexis stopped unexpectedly and caused her grandpa to almost walk into her.

"What is it Lexi?" he asked her.

"I can't believe this place is still here," she said surprised as she looked at a small shop across the street.

"What, you mean Rocky's?"

"Yes. I had completely forgotten about this place until I saw it now."

"Do you want to go in and get something like the old days?" he asked with a smile.

Alexis nodded and they all crossed the street and entered Rocky's. She felt like she was a child again walking into the shop as she looked at all the candy and the counter with freezers full of ice cream. Her grandparents had taken her here when she was little, and she would always get the same thing. She walked over to the counter and looked at all the flavours they had and near the middle they still offered her favourite flavour.

"Sugar cone with two scoops of maple fudge?" her grandpa asked, remembering what her favourite was after all these years.

"Yes please," she said excitedly, just like she had as a child, but she would not make a mess of herself like she had back then. Her grandma would always have to wash her dress afterwards.

Susan laughed at her granddaughter's excitement and a deeper laugh joined hers. She turned to see Jake had entered the store with Becky and he had seen her enthusiasm.

"I'm not sure who's more excited for ice cream, Lexi or Becky?" Jake said with a chuckle.

"Miss Alexis!" Becky called out when she saw her.

"Becky, what are you doing here?" Alexis asked as Becky came over to hug her.

"Daddy promised me ice cream if I finished all my dinner."

"Oh, that was nice of him."

"What flavour are you getting?"

"My favourite one that I used to always get when I was your age, maple fudge."

"Really? That's my favourite one too!"

"Well I guess great minds think alike and like the same things," Alexis said giving the girl an affectionate hug.

"Make that two maple fudge cones," Marty told the clerk behind the counter.

When everyone had gotten what they wanted they left the store and walked back towards The Inn. Becky held Alexis's hand and wouldn't let go.

"It's good to see Becky so happy," Susan commented to Jake who was walking beside her and Marty.

"Yes, it is. She's taken a real liking to Lexi and Lexi to her. I have never known Becky to warm up to anyone like she has to her. She's close to Samantha but it's nothing like this. I wish she had been able to meet Lexi a long time ago," Jake replied and sighed.

"And what about you? Would you have liked to have met Alexis earlier too?"

"Yes."

"I wish you could have too Jake. It seems like you two were destined to be together and you make each other happy. Are there any plans to take this any further?"

"I'm not sure. I mean I do want to, but I want to make sure that this is going to last, not just for my sake but for Becky's as well. I don't want her to get hurt. She's suffered enough pain by not having a mother growing up, and I don't want her to get her hopes up with Alexis if it's not meant to be."

Susan stopped walking and Jake stopped to, as Marty continued to walk behind the others. "Let me ask you this Jake, do you love her?"

"Yes."

"Can you see yourself spending your life with her?"

"Yes."

"Can you imagine life without her?"

"No."

"Than what are you waiting for? She's the one for you. I knew this and that's why I brought her out here." Susan snapped her mouth shut as she realized what she had just revealed to Jake.

"Don't worry Susan, we figured out what you were up to a long time ago," Jake said with a grin. "But I am happy that you did what you did. Not just for me but I think it did Lexi a world of good to come out here too. She's had it rough and Silver Springs was a good place for her to heal."

"I'm glad you're not upset with me for what I did, I only wanted what I thought would be best for you two and I wanted to see you both happy again."

"And we are, thanks to you."

"So, now tell me, are you going to ask my granddaughter to marry you?"

Jake laughed and gave Susan and hug saying, "soon."

Alexis saw Jake and her grandma stop to talk and wondered what the two of them were up to. It ended with him hugging her grandma and both of them smiling. She would have to ask Jake later if she got the chance to. Right now Becky was too busy telling her about how her daddy had told her about the plans to start on the cabin and how excited she was. Apparently, Jake had booked the weekend off and agreed to take her camping up there, so she could see the work being done on the cabin. Alexis listened to the girl chatter away while still wondering what the other two had been talking about.

When the weekend came, Becky was near to bursting in excitement to get to the cabin. She had asked Alexis if she wanted to go but she had declined saying she needed to get some things done and spend some time with her grandparents. Becky was disappointed that she wasn't coming but took it in stride. The girl had tried to persuade her again to come and Alexis had told her to go enjoy a weekend with her dad since he had been spending so much time with her instead lately. Becky agreed but made her promise that they would have dinner together Sunday night when they got back.

After they left Alexis cleaned her cabin and aired it out before making herself some dinner. Afterwards she curled up on the sofa and read her book until she fell asleep. The next day she spent some time going over last-minute details for the anniversary party and then went for lunch with her grandparents. They had decided on a picnic in the park like they had done when she was younger, and they talked for hours. Alexis realized just how much she had missed them over the years and she cherished this time with them.

Later Alexis went to Sam's to browse while her grandparents stopped in to talk with Mr. Webber. She noticed that they had been talking to him a lot recently and wondered what was going on. She was tempted to ask them, but she decided against it since she knew they would tell her if it was serious. She was standing in the fiction aisle when she overheard two women talking in the next aisle over and it caught her attention.

"Have you heard the news about Jake?" the one woman asked.

"No, what's going on?" the other woman asked?

"I heard that Becky's mom Janice is back in town, and the only reason why she would do that is to get Jake back. Apparently, he met up with her yesterday."

"But it's been almost seven years since she left and ran out on the two of them."

"I know, but I don't think that Jake truly go over her leaving, why else would he have stayed a bachelor all this time?"

"I don't know, but isn't he with that new girl in town, what's her name?"

"I think it's Alexis. I think she's Marty and Susan's granddaughter or something. He's probably only with her so he can stay on good terms with Marty and Susan, or he feels sorry for her. I mean, he's never really dated anyone since Janice and god knows we've all tried to get his attention."

"You really think that's what he's doing?"

"Sure, I mean have you seen her? She's an uptight city girl and you know how he feels about city girls."

"That's true. It will be interesting to see what happens while Janice is in town, when is she supposed to leave?"

"Monday, I think."

"Alexis doesn't have a chance with her here. Jake was head over heals in love with her and she's a knock out. I wish I had her good looks."

"Me too, I always envied her, we all wanted Jake but she's the one that got him."

"I wonder what little miss city girl is going to do when Jake dumps her for Janice? She'll be the laughing stock of the town."

"Yes she will, and I'll bet you anything she'll go running back to the city where she belongs."

Alexis had heard enough by this point and walked quickly out of the store past Samantha who tried to stop her but with no success. She wanted to get back to her cabin before she burst into tears in public. She was halfway down the path that led to the clearing where her cabin was before she broke down. She crumpled to her knees and sobbed. She was heartbroken and felt like her world had come crashing down around her. Now she understood why Jake had never talked about their future together. He was still in love with his ex Janice. She finally managed to pick herself up and ran the rest of the way to her cabin where she collapsed on her bed and cried her heart out. She fell into an exhausted sleep and did not awake again until hours later when knocking on her door woke her up.

She wiped her face and straightened her clothes before opening her door to find her worried grandparents standing outside. She was supposed to have met them for dinner but had fallen asleep.

"Alexis, are you okay? We were so worried about you when you didn't show up for dinner," Susan said entering the cabin.

"I'm sorry Grandma, I fell asleep."

Susan took a closer look at her granddaughter before asking, "have you been crying?"

"Oh Grandma!" Alexis got out before she clung to her and broke down into tears again.

"Lexi, dear, what is it?" her grandpa asked her concerned.

"It's Jake," she managed to get out before she started sobbing again.

Alexis didn't say anything else and only shook her head. Marty and Susan looked at each other worriedly as they had no clue as to what was going on. When Alexis hadn't shown up for dinner they had called Sam's knowing she was going there and had talked to Samantha who had told them what happened in the store. Samantha was as clueless as they were as to what had upset her. Now they find their granddaughter in tears and all they can get out of her was that it had something to do with Jake. As far as they knew nothing had happened to them and Jake had told Susan that he wanted to marry Alexis, so they were stumped.

They stood there and let Alexis cry until she cried herself out and stepped back from her grandma.

"I'm sorry," she sniffled.

"Alexis, please tell us what's wrong," Susan urged.

"I can't, not right now. Is it okay if I stay with you guys for awhile?"

"Of course dear, if that's what you want?"

"Yes, I need to get away from here to think, and I can't do that here."

"Okay. Why don't you pack some things and we'll go home? Maybe later when you're ready you can tell us what happened."

"Thanks Grandma, and I will, but right now I just can't bring myself to talk about it."

Alexis went and got one of her suitcases and packed some of her clothes and toiletries into it. Once done she left with her grandparents and headed back to The Inn where their car was parked. They drove in silence to the condo that they owned in one of the new developments and got her settled into the guest room. Alexis turned down the offer for dinner and told her grandparents that she just wanted to get some sleep. They respected her wishes and kissed her and left her to get some rest. Alexis regretted making them worry over her, but she would make it up to them at a later time. For now she just wanted to sleep and forget today, and possibly the last two months. Exhaustion overtook her, and she fell asleep with the image of Jake and a mysterious women in her mind.

Chapter Sixteen

Alexis awoke late the next day exhausted and with a killer migraine. Her sleep had been restless and unanswered questions kept running through her mind. The one foremost in her mind was, why? Why had Jake pretended to like her if her wasn't over his ex, Janice? Was this why he hadn't talked about their future together, or why he had yet to propose to her? Was he still hoping to reunite with Janice? Another big question was, why had he not told her he had met with her on Friday? The answer to that one was obvious, he still cared and wanted Janice and now that she was back, he would forget about her.

Now that she thought about it, on Friday Becky had been the one pleading for her to go camping with them whereas Jake had said nothing. He had just kissed her goodbye and said he would see her on Sunday. Was he planning to break up with her then. Well she would just save him the time and her more heart ache by ending it herself. She should have known that he would turn out like all the other men she had known, they were all the same deep down inside she thought.

Alexis padded out of her room in her slippers and pajama's in search of coffee and some Advil. She found both in the kitchen and a note from her grandparents saying that they had to go out and would be back later and to make herself at home. Home. She didn't really have a home right now. But she would have to remedy that situation soon and she wasn't sure it was going to be here in Silver Springs.

Seeing Jake with another woman would kill her and she wanted to avoid it.

Deciding she had nothing better to do she went back to her room and climbed back into bed. She was determined that she was not going to cry again and that she had shed enough tears over what had happened. She was a survivor and she would survive this. She had survived worse over the years. She told herself this over and over as she drifted off to sleep again.

Alexis woke up a few hours later to the sound of voices coming from the living room. She could hear her grandparents talking to someone else and she wondered who it could be. A few minutes later someone knocked softly on her door and she called out to whoever it was to come in, she assumed it would be her grandma. Instead it was Samantha who came in and shut the door, then went over to sit on the edge of the bed.

"I came by to make sure that you were okay," Samantha said kindly. "I saw you leave the store upset yesterday and when you didn't answer me I was worried something had happened. Your grandparents are worried too and when they asked me what happened I had no clue as to what to tell them. They've asked me to come over and see if you want to talk to me about what's got you so upset."

"I appreciate you coming by, you're a true friend. But I don't think I'm ready to talk about it yet if you don't mind," Alexis responded quietly.

"If that's what you want, I'll respect your wishes. But know that you have friends here and we're here to help you if you need it."

"Thank you Samantha, it warms my heart to know that there are good people like you out there."

"I'm here anytime you need me Alexis."

Alexis leaned over and gave her friend a hug and decided since Samantha had been kind enough to come by and see to her well being that she should at least get up and visit with her for awhile. She told Samantha that she would be out shortly as she wanted to take a quick shower. When she entered the living room a short while later she found that not only were her grandparents and Samantha there, but Brian was as well.

"Hello Alexis," Brian greeted her as she entered the room.

"Hi Brian, I didn't know that you were here too," Alexis said, self conscious of the way she looked right now. She had thrown on track pants and a t-shirt and had left her hair wet, plus she was wearing no make up.

"Don't worry, you still look beautiful the way you are," Brain told her as if he had read her mind.

Alexis blushed at this and sat down next her grandma on one of the sofas. "It was nice of you two to come and see me," she said, not knowing what else to say.

"We were both worried about you and when Marty and Susan asked Sam to come over, I decided to come tag along too to make sure you were okay."

"That was very kind of you. As I was saying to Samantha earlier, I am truly lucky to have you all as friends. I'm sorry to have worried you all but for now I need to deal with what I'm going through on my own. I hope you don't think that I'm being rude, but I just need some time while I sort everything out and what I'm going to do, and I guess where I'm going to live."

"Live? What do you mean dear?" Susan asked.

"I mean, I'm not sure if I'm going to say in Silver Springs Grandma."

"But where would you go, and more importantly why would you leave? I thought you liked it here and what about Jake, and Becky?"

At the mention of Jake's name, Alexis's eyes started to tear up and she tried desperately not to break down in front of them. Everyone looked at one another in confusion as they all realized that Jake was definitely the source of her unhappiness. Susan wrapped her arms around her granddaughter and held her close. She didn't know what was going on and she was hesitant to ask since Alexis had just told them all that she needed time before she shared what was happening. She looked to her husband for support and Marty seemed at a loss as to what to do, just like her.

Alexis leaned into her grandma and she lost her battle to not cry and wept in her grandma's arms. She tried to gain control but couldn't and abruptly stood up and excused herself then fled to her room. Everyone was shocked to see her go and no one said a word not knowing what to say or think. They sat there for a few minutes and it was Brian who finally broke the silence.

"I think maybe I should go talk to Jake and see if he knows what's going on. I don't think we're going to get any answers out of Alexis for awhile and I think it's safe to say that whatever is troubling her has to do with Jake," he stated as he stood up.

"Do you want me to go with you?" Samantha asked standing up as well.

"No, I think you should stay here in case she needs you."

"Okay, I can stay for awhile, but I need to get back to the store later."

"Sounds good. I'll call you after I talk to Jake, but it may take me some time since he's up at his cabin by Silver Lake."

"Don't worry, just call me when you know something and then maybe we'll know what to do to help Alexis."

Brain gave his wife a kiss on the cheek, then said good bye to Susan and Marty and left. Susan got up saying she was going to make another pot of coffee and then go see if Alexis was hungry since she was sure the girl hadn't eaten yet today, and she had missed dinner last night. She came back to the living room a few minutes later saying Alexis was sleeping again and that she didn't want to disturb her. They sat and talked quietly until around five o'clock when Samantha announced that she needed to head back to her store. She promised to let Marty and Susan know what Brain learned then kissed the elderly couple on their cheeks and left.

Marty and Susan went to prepare dinner, not knowing what else to do. They hoped that Alexis would come out eventually and eat something. To their delight, Alexis did appear later to eat with them, but her appetite was small. She had large bags under her eyes and Susan could not think of a time when her granddaughter had ever looked this sad or beaten. Whatever had happened was taking its toll on Alexis and it wasn't good. After dinner they all watched television, but Alexis did not see what was happening on the television. Her thoughts were else where and she was tired, despite how much sleep she had gotten in the past twenty-four hours. Around nine she bade her grandparents goodnight and retired to her room for the night until the morning.

Jake arrived back at his home early the next morning with Becky, having cut their camping trip short. When Brian had shown up yesterday and told him about Alexis he had become worried and could see why Brian was worried too. Between the two of them, neither of them could come up with an explanation as to what had happened to upset Alexis so much. They had not had a fight and as far as he knew she had been looking forward to having dinner with them Sunday night. When Brain told him that she had mentioned leaving Silver Springs his jaw had dropped. What could make her want to leave so suddenly? He and he had to think of something to convince her to stay as he couldn't imagine not having her here.

He and Brian had talked for a long time while trying to keep what was happening from Becky. The last thing he wanted was his daughter to get caught up in this and get hurt. Although he knew if Alexis left it would devastate the girl, not to mention himself. When Brian had left he had told Becky that they would have to leave in the morning because an emergency had come up at The Inn. He didn't like lying to her, but he felt it was necessary for now to protect her. She had been disappointed as she was having fun watching the crew work on their cabin, but he had promised her that they would come up during the week to check on the progress. They would not be able to come up the following weekend until Sunday as Saturday was Marty and Susan's anniversary party.

Jake unloaded the Jeep while Becky and Max took off down the path to The Inn and he would occasionally look towards the empty cabin that Alexis had been staying in. Brain had told him that she was staying at Marty and Susan's and it seemed empty here without her.

"Daddy, where's Miss Alexis?" Jake heard his daughter yell at him later.

"I don't know Sweat-Pea," he answered her.

"She's not at The Inn and her cabin looks empty."

"Maybe she went into town for a bit," he lied.

"Oh, okay. Hopefully she hasn't forgotten that we're supposed to have dinner together tonight."

"I'm sure she hasn't. Were Grandma Susan and Grandpa Marty at The Inn?" Jake asked her.

"Yeah, they were in their office and they seemed upset about something."

Jake sighed, and he decided that maybe going to talk to them first would be his best course of action before he went to talk to Alexis. "Becky, want to go to Sam's while I get things sorted out?"

"Sure Daddy. Is Grandpa Marty and Grandma Susan being upset why we had to come back early?"

"Yes, that's part of it. Now come on, go get you art supplies and I'll call Samantha to let her know you're coming."

"Okay, be back in a minute!"

Jake called Samantha and spoke with her briefly and could not get anymore information out of her other than what Brian had already relayed to him. Confused, he waited outside for Becky and when she came out they got back into the Jeep and drove into town. After he had dropped Becky off her went back to The Inn and found Marty and Susan in their office talking quietly. When they saw him, they stopped, and Susan quickly got up and went to him and hugged him.

"Oh Jake! I don't know what's wrong with her? She won't talk to any of us about what happened," Susan cried.

Jake hugged her back and he felt sick at the thought of these two wonderful people being heartbroken. He looked to Marty and he saw the worry etched into his face over his granddaughter.

"She wouldn't say anything to you two either?" he finally asked as he led Susan back to the sofa.

"No. All we know is that we had a wonderful time with her in the park on Saturday, then she went to the bookstore. Something must have happened there because Samantha said she left the store upset and everything's just been a mystery since then as to what's got Alexis upset. Jake, she wants to leave Silver Springs!"

"I don't know what to say Susan. I'm as much in the dark as you two are. I came back as soon as I could and thought maybe I should talk to you two before I go see her. Do you think she will see me, since it seems to be the general consensus that this is about me, but I have no idea why?"

"We're not sure," Marty spoke up. "Is there anything you can think of that you might have said or did to make her so upset?"

"Not that I know of. I haven't seen her since Friday and you said she was fine until yesterday afternoon, so I'm baffled because I haven't spoken to her in two days."

"Then maybe someone said something to her at the store yesterday. Did Samantha say if Alexis had spoken to anyone in there?"

"Not that I'm aware of but I'll call her and ask her."

Jake called Samantha and when he got off the phone with her he had a vague idea of what might be happening. If it was what he suspected, then he knew why Alexis was upset.

"What is it Jake?" Susan asked worriedly when she saw the look on his face.

"Samantha said she didn't see Alexis speak to anyone, but she did mention that Kori and Stephanie were in the store and you know how those two are the biggest gossips in town?" Jake muttered the last part.

"Weren't they best friends with Janice?"

"Yes and that would be my problem I'm thinking," Jake sighed and sat down in the nearest chair.

"What do you mean Jake? What could they have to do with this?"

"It's Janice. I didn't tell you this because I didn't want it getting back to Becky, but her mom is in town for the weekend."

"She's what!" Susan exclaimed. "She has some nerve showing her face back in this town after what she did to you and Becky!"

"I know, and I wish she wasn't here either, but she called me last week to ask if I would meet with her."

"Why the hell would she want to meet with you after all these years and why did you agree?" a usually calm Marty exploded.

"It's not what you think. I only agreed to meet with her briefly because her parents were killed in a car accident two weeks ago and in their will they left a few family heirlooms to Becky. Janice was here to give them to me and that's it. So I met with her briefly on Friday to get those things from her and as far as I know she left town either last night or this morning to go back home."

"Oh, well that is unexpected. So what does that have to do with Kori, Stephanie and Alexis?" Susan asked

"My guess is that Alexis overheard a conversation those two were having and if I know Kori, she was probably gossiping and making up stories. She probably said that Janice was back in town because of me and that we might get back together. Kori never could keep her mouth shut or tell the truth."

"Oh Jake, if Alexis heard that she probably thinks that you would go back to Janice and that you never wanted her. Oh my poor girl, no wonder why she's heartbroken and wants to leave town. Jake you have to make this right and go talk to her."

"I plan to right away, but the question will be, will she listen to me. We both know her history with men and she's probably thinking the worst of my gender right now."

"We'll come with you and let me go in first and ask her to talk to you," Susan said getting up and picking her purse up off the desk.

The three of them left, with Marty and Susan taking their car and Jake following them in his Jeep. When they arrived at the condo building Marty and Jake agreed to stay downstairs while Susan went up to talk to Alexis. It was twenty minutes before Susan came back down shaking her head sadly.

"I tried Jake, but she doesn't want to see you. I even tried to explain to her what happened, but she won't listen to me. Apparently, she's already made plans to go stay with the family of her best friend Karla. She told me she's leaving Sunday morning. Oh Jake, we can't let her leave. I don't want to lose her again and she was meant to be with you. We have to come up with something to make her stay and see that she belongs here with all of us."

"But what can we do dear?" Marty asked

"I don't know but there has to be something. I did not have her come all the way out here to fail and have her leave us again. I will think of something," Susan said determined to do just that.

Jake's shoulders slumped at the thought of losing Alexis. For the first time in his life he had found true love and he was about to lose that. His heart felt like it was breaking, and he just didn't know how to deal with all of this.

"Come on Jake, Marty, let's go to the café at Sam's and see if we can figure this out. Maybe Brian and Samantha can come up with something," Susan said heading back to her car.

"Maybe we should meet somewhere else. Becky's at Sam's right now and I don't want her to overhear us. This is going to break her heart if we can't figure out how to make Alexis stay," Jake responded.

"Okay, how about The Bistro. Give Brain a call and see if he and Samantha can meet us over there. I'm sure Racheal can watch the store and Becky for awhile."

Jake climbed into his Jeep and called Brian to let him know what was going on. Brain agreed that they would meet them at The Bistro in ten minutes and then hung up. Jake sat there for a few minutes staring at nothing and feeling like the world was falling apart around him. He had never felt this depressed in his life and it was a new feeling that he didn't like. He finally started the Jeep and drove off to meet the others and see if he could save his future with Alexis.

Alexis stood in the window of her bedroom watching her grandparents talking with Jake down below in the parking lot.

He looked handsome with the sun glinting off his golden-brown hair and she could see even from up where she was that he looked miserable. His shoulders were slumped, and he had his hands stuffed in his jean pockets.

Her resolve almost broke and she wanted to run to him when she saw him sitting in his Jeep a few minutes later staring off at nothing. But before she could act on that impulse he drove away. She turned from the window and sat down on her bed heavily. It was over. She had made it clear to her grandma that she wanted nothing to do with him and that she was leaving on Sunday. She would have left earlier but she could not bring herself to leave before the anniversary party. She at least owed it to them to stay for that after all they had done for her.

She would have to arrange for someone to go get her things from the small cabin as she couldn't bring herself to go there. She didn't want to run into Jake or relive the memories that were there, and there was Becky. She felt horrible that she was doing this to her. She herself was devastated that she would no longer be here for her and she had grown to love the little girl as her own. What this would do to Becky she couldn't imagine, and tears came to her eyes at the thought.

She curled up on the bed and cried once more for the loss of all she had thought she had found here and at the loss of the new friends she had made. She needed Sunday to come quickly so she could leave and try to rebuild her life, again.

Chapter Seventeen

On Friday Alexis was busy with last minute plans for the anniversary party and had no time to think about Jake. Her heart wasn't into what she was doing but she was determined to give her grandparents the best celebration she could. She had been doing most of the planning from the condo as she did not want to risk running into Jake at The Inn. But tomorrow she would have no choice if she was to attend the party.

With Samantha's help they had arranged to have Marty and Susan meet friends for lunch and a movie yesterday while Stan and his crew had delivered and installed the surprise gift that Alexis had had made for them a day earlier than originally planned. It was now covered with a large white tarp and her grandparents had been nagging her to tell them what it was. She had told them to be patient and they had grumbled that Saturday was too far away to wait. Alexis knew that they were joking, and she loved them for their sense of humor as she knew they were trying to cheer her up in their own way.

After lunch she made her way over to Sam's to have coffee with Samantha. She wanted to spend some time with her new friend before she left town in two days. The two women took their coffees and sat on the sofa near the cold fireplace and chatted about the party tomorrow. Alexis was filling in Samantha on what all she had planned for the party when Brian came rushing into the store and over to them.

"Brian, what's wrong," Samantha asked getting up.

"I need Alexis to come with me. I can't get a hold of Jake since he must be out where there's no cell reception or he's not answering. You're both in danger right now. I'll explain in a minute, but we need to get you out of here as soon as possible," Brian said, urging her to follow him.

Alexis was troubled but didn't hesitate to follow him since he was a friend and she trusted him. Once outside he ushered her into his black SUV and Samantha climbed in as well.

"Brian, what's happening, why am I in danger and why is Jake in danger?" Alexis asked as Brian took the road that would lead them out of town.

"It's Ron, he escaped yesterday, and he was screaming that he was coming after the two of you."

"Ron, but how?"

"I don't know all the details but apparently he was being transferred and when they brought him out he had people waiting and they ambushed the officers escorting him. Thankfully none of them were killed, only badly injured but Ron was able to get away. They figure he had help from the inside and from some his old prison friends from his last incarceration."

"I can't believe this is happening. I thought it was all over after they arrested him that day. Where am I going to go that's safe from a lunatic like that man?"

"It's all taken care of. Stephen and Liz are letting us use a room up at the main lodge at the Silver Mountain Ski Resort until they can catch Ron."

"Will I be safe there, and what about Jake, what if you can't find him in time?"

"Don't worry, we'll find him and bring him to the lodge as well. Ron would be a fool to try and go after the two of you there with that many people around, plus we will have people there watching for him just in case."

"I hope you're right Brian, but what about Becky? Shouldn't she stay with us as well?"

"Becky will be fine. Our friends Matt and Maggie have gone to get her, and they are going to keep her at their place until this is over."

They arrived at the resort and Brian ushered Alexis into the main lodge with Samantha following close behind them. Stephen was waiting for them just inside the doors and he took them immediately upstairs to the room that he had ready for her. Liz was inside waiting for them and she hugged Alexis when she saw her.

"Oh Alexis, this is horrible!" Liz cried. "That awful man is out there somewhere and because of that you have to go into hiding now. It's not fair."

Alexis hugged the woman back and felt lucky to have her as a friend. "Thank you for helping me," Alexis said then released her.

"Think nothing of it, you're our friend and we will always be here for you. Here in Silver Springs we look out for one another and we will help you get through this."

Alexis felt tears come unbidden to her eyes at the kindness all these people were showing her. She didn't know how she was going to leave all these wonderful people behind on Sunday. Seeing her distress, Liz took her by the hand and led her to the sofa and gently prodded her to sit down. She then poured a glass of water for Alexis then sat down beside her.

Alexis murmured a thank you then took in her surroundings. It was a beautiful room with a large sitting area and a separate bedroom off the back. It must be one of the suites Brian had mentioned to her before that he wanted her to redo. She sipped her water then placed it on the coffee table and sat quietly, not knowing what else to do.

"Has anyone been able to get a hold of Jake yet?" Brian asked.

"No, his phone is still going to voicemail," Stephen answered.

Alexis wondered why Jake wouldn't be answering his phone and she was afraid that maybe Ron had already found him or was he with Janice. Both thoughts wrenched at her heart and she hoped that he was okay, even if he wasn't hers anymore.

"I'm going to go back to town to see if I can find him and I'm waiting for Stan to call me back to let me know if he's up at Silver Lake," Brian said getting ready to leave.

"Be careful Brian," Samantha said worriedly as she gave her husband a hug and kissed him.

"I will, and I'll call you if I hear anything." He left after that and Samantha went to sit with the other women.

Stephen stayed and with them as he felt that either himself or Brian should be with Alexis at all times. He had tried to urge Liz to stay at home, given her condition, but she had refused saying Alexis needed her. He had learned a long time ago not to argue with her, but he still worried for her safety and the safety of their unborn child. Stephen looked at his wife and admired her beauty, and the glow she seemed to have since becoming pregnant.

"What is it Stephen?" Liz asked when she was him watching her.

"I was just thinking that pregnancy suits you," he replied giving her a loving smile.

"Why thank you."

"So when are you due?" Alexis asked.

"Around Christmas time, he or she will be the perfect Christmas present for Stephen and myself."

"Oh that's perfect, I'm so happy for you two. I wish I could be here to meet the little one," Alexis added sadly.

"Alexis, I know it's not my place ask, but as your friend I'd like to know why you're leaving us? I thought you liked it here?" Liz asked her.

Alexis felt uncomfortable with the subject but considering everything these people were doing to help her and possibly putting themselves in danger, she felt she owed them an explanation.

"I'm leaving because of Jake…"

"We had a feeling he had something to with it, but we don't understand what happened with you two. You two are in love, anyone can see that and if I'm not mistaken, I think a marriage proposal from Jake was going to be coming soon." Liz looked to her husband for confirmation and Stephen nodded his head.

"But that was before Janice showed back up in his life," Alexis said bitterly.

"Janice? What does she have to do with this?" Stephan asked.

Alexis sighed, then told them everything she had heard while she was in Sam's last Saturday. She tried hard not to cry during this.

"Oh, Alexis, I wish you had told me this earlier," Samantha said shaking her head. "I could have saved you so much pain, and Jake as well."

"What do you mean?"

"The two women you overheard were Kori and Stephanie. They are the two biggest gossips in town and have rarely been known to get the truth right, even when it hits them in the face. Not to mention they've both had their eye on Jake since high school, plus they were best friends with Janice. But what you overheard them talking about was only partly true."

"How so?" Alexis asked, her hopes rising.

"Janice was in town on Friday, but she left this morning. Brian told me all about it. Her parents passed away and she was here to give Jake some family heirlooms to give to Becky when the time is right. Jake didn't tell anyone about it because he didn't think anything of it and was happy that he only had to see her briefly on Friday to get the things from her. There are a lot of people in this town who dislike Janice but no one more so than Jake. He would have been happier if she had just mailed him the stuff."

Alexis let what Samantha said sink in and the enormity of what she had just put herself and Jake through because of gossip threatened to tear her apart. She had been so wrong about Jake, he wasn't one of the bad guys. He loved her, and Liz and Stephen had just confirmed that he had wanted to marry her. What an idiot she was. She had just blown the best thing she had ever had as she doubted that Jake would want her after all of this. She bent over and laid her head on her knees and broke out into a miserable sob.

Alexis felt Liz get up and then someone else sat down and strong arms held her. She turned her head and cried her heart out onto Stephens shoulder. Her world was falling apart, and it was all her fault. If she had jus talked to her friends when they had asked her to or let Jake talk to her that day at the condo this could have all been avoided. Instead she had destroyed the best thing she had ever had, and he wasn't here with her, while another lunatic man wanted to kill them both. That was her fault too since Jake had stood up for her that day in the park. If he hadn't then Ron wouldn't be looking for him too. When her tears subsided, Stephen gave her some Kleenex and she tried to clean her tear streaked face.

"What am I going to do?" Alexis asked no one in general.

"I know Jake, he will forgive you, not just because that's the type of man he is, but because he loves you," Samantha answered.

"Do you really think so?"

"Count on it. Just tell him the truth. This is not something that can't be fixed. Besides, you two have to kiss and make up because I don't want to lose my new friend," Samantha stated with a tearful smile.

"Neither do we," Liz answered for herself and Stephen.

"I am so lucky to have all of you. I have never known anyone with bigger hearts than you and I truly hope that I will be able to stay. I love it here in Silver Springs and I love Jake, I just hope he will forgive me."

"He will," Samantha assured her.

They sat there quietly after that, each of them in their own thoughts. It was the ringing of Stephen's cell phone that broke the silence and they all looked to him in anticipation.

"Hello," Stephen answered.

They watched and listened as he talked to whoever was on the phone for about five minutes before he hung up and looked at Alexis.

"What is it Stephen?" Alexis asked nervously.

"That was Brian. It's Jake..."

"What happened? Is he okay?" Alexis asked standing up and fearing the worst.

"He's fine, just a little banged up. Stan called Brian to let him know that Jake was up at the cabin by Silver Lake helping the crew with the renovations. Apparently, Ron showed up there with a gun and there was a fight. Jake won and with the help of the crew they were able to contain him until the authorities arrived. They're on their way to the police station right now and Brian's gone there to meet them. As soon as they finish up there he said that they come here to meet up with all of us."

"He's really okay, you're not sugar coating it?"

"Yes he's fine. Just a few bruises and scratches."

"Oh thank god. I don't know what I would do if I had lost him."

"Don't worry, that ones a fighter and I know he would do anything he had to keep the woman he loves safe."

"He really loves me?"

"More than you know Alexis. You are his better half and he's waited a long time for you to come into his life. He's liked you since you were both teenagers."

"Teenagers? What do you mean by that? I didn't even him know him then."

Stephen sighed and sat down. He figured since he had let this slip out that the might as well tell her, although it should be Jake telling her this. "Jake and Brain told me this that night we had the barbeque at my place a couple of weeks ago. He knew who you were when you were teenagers, but he never had the courage to approach you even though he liked you and wanted to meet you. You were also hanging around with kids that he didn't get along with."

"I never knew that, and I don't even recall seeing him when I was here for visits."

"Yes well, you two almost met but it wouldn't have been under the greatest conditions."

"Really? When was that."

"I know this is a sensitive subject, but remember that day in the woods when Ron happened upon you?"

"Yes."

"Well you remember telling Jake that the reason why you were able to get the upper hand with Ron and get away was because he became distracted by the sound of someone approaching?"

"You mean…?"

"Yes, that was Jake on the path that day with some of his friends. He vividly remembers seeing you fleeing and the state you were in."

"Oh Stephen, you mean I owe my thanks to Jake for that day?"

"Yes, and then some."

"What do you mean?"

"Have you ever wondered why Ron hates Jake so much?"

"I never really thought about it."

"Well it's more than just because of what happened that day in the park this summer. After you fled that day in the woods, Ron friends fled as well, and Jake beat Ron to a pulp for what he did to you."

Alexis gasped as did the other women in the room. "He did that for me?"

"Yes, and he did it again today. From what Stan told Brian, Ron's not looking his best right now and probably never will again."

Alexis's mind reeled with the news of everything Stephen had just told her. It seemed that she owed Jake a lot. He had saved her three times from Ron now, and today he had put his life on the line for her. How could she have ever doubted that he loved her? She was a fool she thought for the second time that day.

"How am I ever going to face him again after everything he's done for me and the way I treated him?"

"Face him as a woman who loves him and wants nothing more than to spend her life with him," Liz told her.

"I can do that, and I will beg for his forgiveness if it comes to that. I will do everything in my power to be the woman he deserves."

Alexis was anxious to see Jake and hoped that they would be here soon. Restless she walked around the room and then went through the bedroom to the balcony beyond. She opened the doors and breathed deeply of the fresh mountain air and looked to the town in the valley below. This is where she wanted to be, here in Silver Springs, not some city that she no longer loved, or thought she had loved. She vowed to herself that she would throw herself at the mercy of Jake and pray that he forgave her. She leaned against the rail and closed her eyes to wait.

Chapter Eighteen

It had been a long day and Jake felt worse than he looked. The ordeal with Ron had taken its toll on him and his anxiety over Alexis had him to the point where he was exhausted. It had taken him longer than expected at the police station to file his report along with the rest of Stan's crew that had been with him. He wanted nothing more than to go and make sure Alexis was safe, but he did not know if she would want to see him.

He and Brian arrived at the Silver Mountain Ski Resort at the same time that Marty and Susan did. Upon seeing him, Susan rushed up to him and hugged him.

"My poor boy, are you okay? I was so frightened that something had happened to you," Susan exclaimed with tears in her eyes.

"I'm fine Susan. It's over now and Ron will never be able to hurt me or Alexis again. He'll be going away for life this time," he responded, hugging her back.

"That isn't enough for that maniac. He should get the death penalty for what he's put you two through and trying to kill you today!"

"Now dear, you need to calm down," Marty said laying his hand on her shoulder. Ron will get what's coming to him."

"He better, he can't do this to my family and not pay for it."

"Don't worry, he will.   Now let's go make sure our granddaughter is okay."

The four of them entered the resort together and followed Brian up to the room where everyone was waiting for them. Upon entering, Jake was smothered with hugs and kisses from Samantha and Liz, but Alexis was no where to be seen.

"She's out on the balcony," Stephen said when he saw Jake looking around for her. "Go to her, she needs you. We will all wait downstairs in the restaurant for you." Stephen lay his hand on his friend's shoulder and squeezed it in encouragement.

"But shouldn't we see Alexis first?" Susan asked as the others tried to usher her out of the room.

"Let Jake see her first dear," Marty said taking her hand. "Let them straighten things out first and then we can see her after."

"Are you sure?"

"Yes dear."

Susan relented and followed the others out the door but not before giving Jake a smile of encouragement. Once the door shut Jake made his way through the bedroom to the balcony where he could see Alexis standing. She looked beautiful there and he stood there and watched her for a moment before he joined her outside.

Alexis heard someone approach her and she knew instinctively that it was Jake. Opening her eyes she looked at Jake and saw that his handsome face was bruised, and his hair was a mess. Her heart broke for him and she didn't know what to say so instead she threw her arms around him and held him close. She felt him hesitate for only a split second before he crushed her to him.

"I was so scared for you, I thought Ron might find you and kill you," she sobbed into his shoulder.

"And I for you. Even though I knew you didn't want me I couldn't let anything happen to you, not again," Jake said hoarsely.

"Oh Jake, why didn't you tell me about that day in the woods so many years ago?"

"I didn't want you to think less of me for what I did to Ron. I wanted to kill him that day for what he did to you and if it wasn't for my friends I may have."

"Oh Jake, I could never think any less of you. You are a wonderful man and you did what you thought was right at the time. I just wished I had known it was you that day, so I could have thanked you."

"It's the past. What matters now is where we go from here," he said searching her face for answers.

"Jake, I owe you an apology. I acted rashly and, in the process hurt both of us and I should have trusted in you and not thought the worst of you."

"What do you mean Lexi?" Jake asked wiping the tears from her face.

Alexis related what had happened last Saturday and how she had been so wrong to act the way she had. "I hope that you will find it in your heart to forgive me because I want nothing more than to spend the rest of my life making this up to you and showing you that I am the woman for you."

"I already know that you are and there's nothing to forgive. I should have told you about Janice and why she was here. Instead you had to hear it through the worst possible way and it is I who should be apologizing to you."

"Oh Jake, what a pair we make!"

Jake smiled as he realized that things were going to work out between them and he was elated. He lowered his head and kissed her and pulled her close to him once more.

"I love you Lexi and I always will," he breathed between kisses.

"And I love you Jake!"

Alexis groaned as Jake deepened he kiss, and she kissed him back with as mush passion as he could give him. Jake hands were everywhere, he wanted to touch all of her. Impatient, he picked her up in his arms and strode back into the bedroom where he lay her on the bed. She looked up at him with passion filled eyes and waited for him to come to her.

Jake stripped off his clothes then hers and lowered himself down to her. He kissed her stomach and then made his way over every inch of her body. By the time he was done she was moaning to him to take her. Satisfied that he had her where he wanted her, he entered her slowly and felt her clench around him.

"Easy Lexi, or this will be over before I can start," he groaned.

He felt her relax and he held himself still for a moment before he started moving slowly within her. She matched his pace and he leaned down to kiss her on her swollen lips. They moved in perfect rhythm and soon they were lost in the throws of passion and when their climaxes hit, they were so intense that neither of them could move afterwards.

They lay in bed afterwards talking about their future and Jake promised that he was going to marry her as soon as possible, he just wanted to talk to Becky first. Alexis laughed at this.

"What's so funny?" he asked propping himself up on his elbow and looked down at her.

"Becky has been waiting for this to happen just as much as my grandma has. I don't think that you'll run into any problems with her," Alexis stated.

"That is true. Then consider this a pre-proposal, as I don't have your ring on me."

"My ring?"

"Yes, I have a ring that I picked out for you last week at home."

"Really? Oh Jake you bought that last week and then I left you. I'm so sorry!"

"It's okay, we were all working on a plan to keep you here and for me to win you back."

"Really, all of you?"

"Of course. I wasn't about to lose you and your friends didn't want to lose you either. They all love you just like I do, and we will do anything to keep you here. You're a part of Silver Springs just like the rest of us."

"I feel so humbled by all of this. I never knew that I would end up having such wonderful friends like them and to meet a man like you. I am truly grateful to have, and I love you so much."

"I love you too."

"Umm Jake…"

"Yes?"

"What happened to my pre-proposal?"

Jake laughed then said seriously. "Alexis, would you do me the honour of becoming my wife, best friend and soul-mate?"

"Yes Jake, and you will be those things to me as well, forever."

Alexis and Jake joined the others in the restaurant an hour later. They would have joined them sooner but after Jake's pre-proposal, they had made love again and then taken the time to shower and clean up before joining the others. They had entered hand and hand and everyone at the table was grinning.

"I see the two love birds have finally decided to join the rest of us," Brian teased.

Alexis blushed but she was happy and didn't care that they were teasing them. It was obvious that they all knew what they had been doing up in the room, but she was on cloud nine and engaged to the man she loved so no amount of teasing could ruffle her feathers. Alexis noticed that Becky was there now too, and she smiled down at the little girl that she also loved.

"So Daddy, did you finally ask Miss Alexis to marry you?" Becky asked point blank.

Everyone else looked to the couple awaiting the answer.

"Yes Sweet-Pea, I did ask her, and she said yes," Jake answered.

"It's about time Daddy! I thought Grandma Susan and I were going to have to come up with a new plan to get you two engaged since you were taking so long."

Everyone laughed at Becky's directness and Jake leaned down to hug his daughter.

"Looks like yours and Susan's little plan worked although I think that Lexi and I did a good job without your help."

"You mean you knew what we were up to?"

"Yes, we figured it out a long time ago."

Becky smiled at her daddy then turned to Alexis. "Does this mean that I can call you Mom now that you're going to marry my daddy?" she asked pointedly.

"I would be honoured to have you call me Mom," Alexis answered.

"Yes! I finally have a Mom. I've wanted one my whole life and I knew you were going to be the one the day I met you."

"Truly?"

"Yes. I knew you would make the perfect mom and that you were the one daddy has been waiting for."

"Oh Becky, you truly are one of a kind and I love you."

"I love you too, Mom."

Alexis hugged the child and there were tears in everyone's eyes around the table.

Stephen cleared his throat and was the one to speak first. "I think this calls for a celebration. I'm going to have them get my best bottle of champagne from the cellar and we'll toast the happy couple and to good friends."

Everyone cheered to that and they celebrated for many hours afterwards. It was late when they all returned home, and Alexis was elated that everything had worked out and that she would be able to stay in Silver Springs with Jake.

The next day was sunny and warm and they couldn't have asked for better weather for the big party. The Inn was alive with activity as everyone prepared for that evening and the caterers set up the buffet in the newly decorated restaurant. A large tent had been pitched the day before where tables and a bar had been set up, along with a dance floor and live band." By five o'clock Alexis had everything ready and she stood at the front door of The Inn, wearing a black cocktail dress and the beautiful diamond engagement ring that Jake had given her last night, along with an official proposal. Jake stood beside her looking handsome in his black suit and was holding her hand. They were waiting for Susan and Marty to arrive and then they would escort them to the back where everyone was waiting.

Jake kissed the back of her hand and murmured that she looked ravishing and couldn't wait to get her home later. Alexis blushed and replied that she was looking forward to it as well.

Marty and Susan arrived a few minutes later with Becky and they greeted each other with hugs and kisses. Becky took both Alexis's hand and Jake's in hers and they walked together with Marty and Susan out to the back.

Susan's breath was taken away when she saw how much work Alexis had put into her anniversary party and the flowers and fairy lights made the place look magical.

"Alexis, this is beautiful, you are a wonder and how you got all of this done without me knowing is impressive. Marty and I are lucky to have you and we love you so very much," Susan said teary eyed as she and Marty hugged their granddaughter.

"You're welcome Grandma, and I can't take all the credit. Jake did a lot of the planning as well."

"We know, and we thank you as well Jake, for everything," Marty was the one to say.

"You're welcome. I can't think of a more deserving couple than you two to have everyone come out and celebrate your special day," Jake replied.

"One day it will be you two celebrating your fiftieth anniversary and know that even though we won't be here, that we will be there with you in spirit," Susan said with emotion and Jake and Alexis smiled back at her.

"Come, let's go celebrate and greet our guests," Marty said taking his wife by the hand and entering the tent. "It looks like Jake and Alexis have half the town here to see us!"

Susan laughed and followed her husband as they greeted their guests and a waiter gave both of them a glasses of champagne.

"You pulled it off Lexi, I don't think I've ever seen them this happy before, except maybe when they found out you were moving here," Jake stated as he pulled her into his arms and hugged her.

"They deserve this, and I hope that they have many more happy years together. They are an inspiration to me and I hope that you and I are half of what they are."

"We will be, this I promise you."

They watched Marty and Susan for a moment then they went and joined their friends at a small table. Samantha, Brian, Liz and Stephen were all there, and they enjoyed the festivities with much laugher and smiles.

After dinner an eager Susan came to Alexis and asked if they could finally see their surprise that Alexis still had covered with a white tarp. Alexis laughed and agreed and took both her grandparent's hands and walked with them to the large tarp as Jake announced to everyone that Susan and Marty were going to open their gift. Everyone gathered around to watch as Stan, Brain and Jake pulled the tarp off to reveal a hand-crafted gazebo, with intricate wood work and stained to maintain its beautiful natural colour. Susan was speechless, and Marty was as well.

"It's gorgeous and the details are amazing," Susan was finally able to say.

"This is a priceless gift," Marty added.

"I'm glad you both like it. I want to show you something inside," Alexis said leading them into it.

There was a beautiful hand made bench swing, complete with a back and cushions on one side. But what Alexis showed them was above it. Burnt into the beam above were Marty and Susan's names with the date that they had been married. Once again her grandparents were speechless, and they could only hug her with tears in their eyes.

"I love you both," Alexis said affectionately.

"And we love you," they both answered.

The rest of the guests started to come in and take a look and when they all had passed through Marty and Susan announced that they had a special announcement to make. Once again everyone gathered around and waited. Marty was the one to speak.

"Susan and I would like to thank you all for coming to join us on this special day and we have something that we have been waiting a while to tell everyone. Susan and I have decided that it is time for us to retire and to start a new chapter in our life. We have decided to give up The Inn and settle in Mexico for our golden years."

"What! What do you mean Gramps? You can't give up The Inn. This place is your pride and joy and I can't imagine anyone owning what you have spent years to build," Alexis said upset by the news.

"It was a hard decision to make but it's something we feel we need to do," Marty continued.

"But who will own The Inn if you're selling it Gramps?"

Marty smiled at Alexis first then Susan who nodded her head to him.

"Alexis, it has always been our dream for you to come back to Silver Springs and you're Grandma found the perfect opportunity for you to come back to us this year. As you know she had this wild idea that she should play matchmaker and that you and Jake would make the perfect couple. I was hesitant at first but after I saw you two together I saw that your Grandma was right. It was then that we decided we knew what we needed to do."

"I'm confused Gramps, what do Jake and I have to do with this?"

"When you and Jake announced last night that you were engaged, you're Grandma and I went to Mr. Webber this morning to finalize the papers that we had put together last month. As a wedding gift to you both, we are leaving The Inn to you. We know how much this place means to you both and we couldn't bear the thought of strangers owning this place. You and Jake will become the new owners on the day that you two get married."

Alexis stared at her grandparents speechless, as was Jake and almost everyone one else there. Jake looked to Alexis and she looked back trying to comprehend what her grandpa had just said. Her and Jake would own The Inn. When it finally sank in she turned to her grandparents and hugged each of them with tears in her eyes. It seemed all she ever did anymore was cry, but this time it was tears of joy.

"I don't know what to say. This is a gift beyond what words can express. You're right though, I love this place and Jake and I will cherish this gift you have given us," Alexis promised.

"Thank you, Marty, and Susan, I don't know what to say but what Alexis just said. We will accept this gift with the promise that you come back to visit as often as you can and for Christmas. You can't have a hot Christmas on the beach when you can have the beautiful mountains and lots of snow here with us," Jake joked.

"It's a deal," Marty and Susan agreed.

"Come, I think's it's time to celebrate and more champagne is in order!" Jake announced.

The rest of the night passed with stories, many toasts and dancing to the live band. Later that night Jake and Alexis made their way to the gazebo and sat down on the swing together.

"This has turned out to be the perfect night," Alexis sighed as she leaned into Jake.

"Yes it has, and the gift your grandparents gave us is incredible. I'm still in shock over it."

"Me too. It will be a great place for us to raise Becky together and our own children. I want them to love this place as much as I did as a child."

"And they will, with both of us there by their sides to teach them the beauty and magic of The Inn."

"I am so happy that I took the chance to come here when Grandma asked me to. My life will forever be better for it and I now have you and Becky to spend my life with. I couldn't imagine a more perfect life than that."

"I can't imagine my life without you in it. Before you I thought I would never meet anyone to settle down with and that the woman for me didn't exist. Then you walked into my life and turned it upside down and I knew right away that you were the one I had been waiting for. I waited a long time for you and it was worth every minute of the wait."

"I love you Jake. I fought it at first but like you, I knew you were the one. You have made me so happy and I promise to cherish what we have until the end of days."

"I love you too Lexi."

They sat there and looked out over the lake and knew that their journey together was just beginning.

Epilogue

Alexis sat back while Jake put more logs in the wood burning stove. It was a cool night in the mountains as it was the end of September and fall had arrived. They were at their cabin by Silver Lake and they planned to stay there for weekend before leaving for Hawaii for seven days for their honeymoon then back to the cabin for a few days before returning home.

Earlier today they had been married in a quiet ceremony at The Inn. Only their closest friends and family had been invited. Although more people had wanted to attend, Jake and Alexis had agreed they didn't want a huge affair for the ceremony, but they had thrown a large reception afterwards at The Inn for those who wanted to attend.

The gazebo that Alexis had had made for her grandparents anniversary had been decorated with her favourite white lilies and they had held the ceremony in there. Brain had stood up as Jake's best man and Samantha had stood up as Alexis's matron of honour. Becky had been elated to be a flower girl and given the responsibility of holding the wedding bands. Stephen and Liz had also attended along with Marty and Susan and Alexis's mom who had flown in for the wedding. Alexis couldn't have asked for a more perfect day and would remember it forever.

The reception afterwards had been a lively event held in the banquet hall on the third floor of The Inn. A huge buffet had been set up and anyone who wanted to stop by was welcome to. There was also dancing with a live DJ and Alexis felt that at one-point half the town was crammed into The Inn. Alexis hadn't realized that the two of them were that popular and well liked by the towns residents and was touched by how many people had come to congratulate them and wish them well. She had danced and laughed with Jake and when they cut the cake she had made sure he wore a good portion of it on his face.

By ten o'clock, Alexis and Jake made their exit with Alexis throwing her bouquet of white lilies and Becky being the one to catch it. Becky had been thrilled to be the one to catch it and Alexis suspected that the other women had let the little girl have it. They had left in Jake's Jeep which the guys had gaudily decorated and headed out to the cabin on Silver Lake. Becky would stay with Marty and Susan for the next twelve days and shortly after that Marty and Susan would be heading to Mexico to begin their retirement there.

Alexis and Jake were still in shock of having been left The Inn and today Mr. Webber had had them sign all the legal documents to transfer the title deed over to them. It had been a tearful moment for Marty and Susan as they handed over The Inn, but there were also tears of joy for knowing that The Inn was in good hands with their family that loved the place as much as they did.

Now it was nearing midnight and Jake and Alexis were settled into the newly renovated cabin and were curled up on the sofa in front of the fire. Jake was proud of how the cabin had turned out and when he had suggested that they stay there the weekend before their honeymoon, Alexis had been all over it. She loved the place just as much as he did, and she looked forward to these couple of days of solitude with him.

"Mrs. Forester, I would have to say that for someone who just got married today that you have too many clothes on for our wedding night!" Jake teased as he kissed her neck.

Alexis laughed and playfully punched him in the arm. "The same could be said about you Mr. Forrester," she shot back.

"Well that can be easily fixed," he said pulling them both up and peeling off her shirt.

Both of them had changed out of their wedding attire before leaving The Inn as to not ruin Alexis's beautiful dress and Jakes custom tailored suit.

"No way, you first," Alexis said as he tried to rid her of her bra.

"Now how is that fair?"

"It's not, but I want to see the gorgeous man I married naked before you strip me of my clothes and have your way with me!"

"Well, if you insist," he answered undoing his shirt.

Alexis stopped him as she wanted to be the one to undress him. She took her time and by the time she was done Jake stood there in the firelight looking magnificent. Alexis trailed her hands over his muscular arms and lean stomach. She wanted to touch every inch of him and taste him. She proceeded to do just that, and Jake was barely able to keep himself standing with what she was doing to him,

"Lexi, that's not fair," he finally growled bringing her to stand up against him. He was on fire and about to lose control.

Alexis smiled mischievously at him and he lowered his head and kissed her with fervor. She clung to him and he wanted to feel her skin against him, not her clothes. Impatiently he stripped her of her clothes and subjected her to the same treatment she had just lavished on him. When she could no longer stand he lowered her to the blankets spread on the floor in front of the fire and kissed her like there was no tomorrow.

Jake pulled back to take a deep breath and tried to control his rampaging body. This was their wedding night and he didn't want to completely ravage her the first time around. He had all night to do that. He leaned back down and kissed her slowly this time, wanting to savour the taste of her and then he entered her slowly. He could feel Alexis's excitement and he knew she was nearing her brink as well. He held still for a long minute before gently making love to his new wife.

His wife. Jake loved the sound of that and he could still hardly believe that he had found his soul mate after all these years and that she had been more than he had ever dreamed that woman would be. To him Alexis was his other half and he would cherish every moment they spent together for the rest of their lives.

Jake felt the growing excitement within Alexis and he held back no more. The two of the clung desperately as their love making became frenzied and they both climaxed together. When they both could finally breath again they rolled to their sides and Jake lay behind her and held her close. They watched the fire as their breathing slowed and they fell asleep that way until they awoke to make love again several times throughout the night.

The next morning Jake brought coffee outside to where Alexis was standing looking out over the mountains. The trees had changed colour already and the geese were heading south for the winter. The sky was crystal blue with not a cloud to be seen. She couldn't have asked for a more perfect fall morning and wanted to enjoy the nice weather while she could. Jake handed her a mug of coffee and they stood there quietly enjoying the peaceful morning.

"This is what I remember of my time here in the mountains as a child. The beauty of the mountains and the peaceful serenity you can find here. Thank you for showing me the beauty of this place again Jake. For too many years I was in the dark, alone and hating the world. You have shown me what it means to live and what beauty the world holds," Alexis said wrapping her arm around him.

"You're welcome Lexi. From the day I met you I knew I had found the woman I had been searching for my whole life. You were a feisty city girl but under all of that you had a kind heart and you showed my daughter a kindness that very few people ever have. I love you even more for that alone."

"You and Becky are the best thing to ever happen to me and I will always cherish you both. You are my family and with you is where my heart belongs."

"And you have had my heart all this time, you may have even stolen it when were teenagers even though we didn't know each other. Maybe that's why I could never find anyone because my heart knew that you were the one for me and it was waiting for you to come back."

Alexis turned to Jake and looked up into his handsome face. "I love you Jake Forrester, now and forever."

"And I love you Alexis Forrester, now and forever."

Alexis heart skipped a beat at the sound of her new name and she kissed Jake with all the love she had to show him. She would never be in the dark and alone again, with Jake in her life she could only see a bright future full of happiness and love. Now that was something she could live with…

The Lodge at Silver Lake

(Book Four of the Silver Springs Collection)
Coming soon...

The newly-weds were sitting on their porch enjoying a quiet evening to themselves the day after their return from Hawaii, when headlights coming through the trees caught their attention.

"I wonder who that could be?" Jake muttered.

Alexis wondered the same thing because everyone knew they were still on their honeymoon, plus who would come out here this late at night? Unless it was an emergency. The first thought that came to her mind after that was Becky. Had something happened to Jakes daughter and her new step-daughter. She stood up hoping that wasn't the case.

The headlights stopped at the edge of the clearing and didn't come any closer. Jake had recently had the small cabin renovated and while doing that he had had the dirt driveway leveled out and extended to the cabin, when it had once ended where the strange car had just stopped.

They watched as someone got out of the car and it appeared to be a man. It was dark, so they couldn't tell if it was anyone they knew.

"Hello!" Jake called out to the stranger.

The stranger didn't say anything and stood there for a moment then started walking towards them. Alexis slid closer to Jake unsure of what to make of the situation and after recent events was a little cautious. She felt Jake lay a hand on the small of her back and it helped comfort her. In moments the stranger's face came into view and Alexis could see that he was young, maybe a few years older than her, and handsome in his own way.

"Hi," he said as he reached the bottom of the porch steps. "My name's Ethan, and I think I'm lost."

"Well Ethan, it's nice to meet you. I'm Jake and this is my wife Alexis. Where is it you were trying to get to?"

"My friend Brian from Silver Springs suggested a place for my friends and I to go fishing for a week and I was late in coming so I had to come by myself. The place is called The Lodge and it's on Silver Lake."

"You're definitely lost then because you took the wrong turn off the highway to end up here instead of at The Lodge. But we can give you directions there, it's not too far from here."

"I appreciate it. It's so easy to lose your way up here in the dark, I hope I can find it."

"Wait a minute, you said Brain. Do you mean Brian Townsend?" Alexis asked.

'Yes that's him, do you know him?" Ethan asked.

"He's one of our closest friends," Jake answered. "How do you know him?"

"We were roommates when he was living in New York for a time and we've been good friends ever since. I moved to Surrey a few years ago and he helped me buy my home there," Ethan informed them.

"Ethan. Why does that name sound familiar?" Jake asked.

"Does your last name happen to be Bennett?" Alexis asked

"Yes it is," Ethan replied.

"So you're EB. We've heard a lot about you!" Alexis exclaimed excitedly.

Ethan groaned when he heard that. "Is Brian still calling me by my initials?"

"Yes, why don't you like it?"

"I don't mind it, it's just that I didn't realize that he referred to me that way to his friends."

"Why's that?" Alexis asked curiously.

"It's a long story and I'm very tired right now. Is it okay if I told you another time?" Ethan asked heavily.

"Oh, all right, no worries and I understand. Why don't you come in for a few minutes and Jake can give you directions to where you need to go?"

"I'd appreciate that, you two are very kind."

Alexis was excited as Ethan followed them into the cabin. She had known a few celebrities in her time in Toronto but none of them were of interest her, but here was one that she had wanted to meet for a long time. To meet Ethan Bennett was a dream come true. She couldn't wait to talk to him some more, but she would have to contain her excitement and wait since her and Jake were still on their honeymoon after all. Hopefully she would get a chance to talk to him while he was here on vacation with his friends. She closed the door behind them and still could not believe that Ethan Bennett was in her home...

Tima S. Dowding currently resides in Edmonton Alberta, Canada, with her husband, sons, and her dogs. She's a former Wedding and Special Events Planner, and in the past, has donated much of her time to volunteer work in the public schools and the Autism Society.

Tima stays at home full time now to raise her young Autistic son and writes in her spare time. She enjoys golfing, camping, going to the mountains and sitting back to relax with a glass of wine with her husband or to read a good book. Her favourite authors are Terry Goodkind and John Saul.

Tima has always had a passion for writing and was encouraged by her favourite teacher to write. With a soft spot for romance, she took her love of writing and wrote her first book Silver Mountain which she Self-Published in 2017. She also enjoys writing poetry and hopes to one day publish a book of her favourite works.

Tima is currently working on book four and it will be available soon. For Tima's full Bio and information, visit her website at:

timasdowding.wixsite.com/mysite

*If you enjoyed this book, please leave a review on Amazon!

9 781989 129036